To Kill a Cardinal

To Kill a Cardinal

Michael Rumaker

Arthur Mann Kaye, Publisher

SECOND PRINTING

Copyright (c) 1992 by Michael Rumaker

LCCN 92-72298 / ISBN 0-9632962-2-1

When Peter The Poet, frantically pacing the sagging floor of his squalid squatter's flat down on lower Manhattan's Avenue D, thought of the smoke-blue semi-automatic pistol he kept hidden up on the top shelf of the roach-infested cupboard in his dark hole of a kitchen, it filled him, in these sleepless pre-dawn hours, with a feeling of dread.

Underlying this gut-wrenching feeling was, however, a curious sense of comfort: one of the bullets in its loaded chamber had, emblazed in clear script across his frenzied poetic mind's eye so that it all but singed his bloodshot eyeballs, the name of The Cardinal written on it—or, to put it more precisely, being a poet and prone to excess, he saw *every* bullet in the semi-automatic's chamber with The Cardinal's name inscribed upon it, just in case The Poet, no marksman, missed that morning with the first shot.

Meanwhile, at that very same hour, in a very different neighborhood uptown on Madison Avenue behind the vast Cathedral, The Cardinal himself had just moments before risen from a peaceable sleep beneath the canopy of his four-poster bed in his gloomy, still-dark bedroom in his suite of rooms on the second floor of The Chancellory.

First blessing himself and muttering a prayer of thanks to God for having seen fit to let him open his eyes on yet another morning, he pulled his undershirt over his head and tossed it aside, then slipped his bony size 12's into a pair of well-worn slippers and hoisted his tall, gaunt frame off the bed with a groan. Padding across yards of silken carpet, he swung open the vast oaken door

1

of his bath, clicked on the light—an antique gas mantle wired many years back when electricity had first been installed in the Cardinals residence—and dragged his soles across the worn tiles to the huge ancient toilet raised on its marble platform.

The Cardinal unsnapped his clerical-black boxer shorts and let them, as always, slide down no further than his kneecaps as he lowered himself onto the oak toilet seat—Worn smooth by how many cardinals' bottoms? he wondered. Wood was so much more pleasant, he sighed, to one's bare posterior the first thing in the morning; unlike the cold, hard ersatz mother-of-pearl plastic seat he had sat on morning after morning in the bishop's residence in Camden, New Jersey, before, glory be to God, The Pope had given him his red hat.

He pulled from the linen shelf within hand's reach of the commode his leather breviary, given to him by his Sainted Mother on the day of his ordination as a priest so many years ago, its covers now worn to a sensuous suppleness.

"Time to get in a bit of me morning prayers," he murmured, as he always did each dawn at this time, for he had an unusually busy schedule every day, and had to make use of every odd moment. Even though it was a Sunday morning, it was still a "working day" for him, his most important, for in a few hours he would be saying high mass in The Cathedral and delivering the homily he'd been working on all week, just as he did every blessed Sunday of the year.

"There are no holidays in God's house," he was fond of saying.

As his lips fluttered in prayer, he gazed, still admiringly and with a feeling of satisfaction and gratitude, just as he had when he'd first sat "on the throne"—a jape of a euphemism, learned as a child from his Sainted Mother—here in The Chancellory bathroom that cold winter morning several years back. His eyes, as always, started with the dark paneled wood of the vaulted ceiling, then slid down the equally dark wainscoting of the upper walls to the gray marbled portion beneath, where one tiny slot of a stained glass window of the Virgin Mary had been inserted, and where the wan light of a Manhattan dawn showed amidst the cobalt blues of her gown in the cut glass; his gaze ending at the worn octagonal white tiles of the floor.

"How many feet have trudged these tiles?" he wondered.

Pausing in his reading, The Cardinal studied, as he often did, the path worn to "the throne," giving him a powerful reminder of tradition, like the traditional path of The Church itself, worn deeply, unwaveringly, unceasingly over the centuries.

Perhaps there was a metaphor in that, he thought, for his homily that morning, and he reached behind for the pen and note pad he always kept on top of the water tank and scratched a hasty note to himself.

Now his eyes shifted to the ancient tub with its heavy antique hardware, thick metal spigots a hand could really grasp, where the water was steaming in a bath drawn earlier by Brother Francis while The Cardinal slept, so that by the time The Cardinal got through shaving the temperature would be just right.

Now there was a tub, he sighed with satisfaction, as always, as he gazed down its comfortable long length, a tub a man could stretch his legs in and still have room to spare, a man such as The Cardinal himself, who was just over six feet tall.

3

He lay his breviary aside.

"Ahhhhh," he breathed. The first turd was always a bit of a strain, accompanied by a bit of a pain, too. He wondered if it was a touch of the hemorrhoids returning. Ran in the family, they did . . . his Sainted Mother especially, always tormented by them . . . But he did not like to think about that, especially of those suppositories, slippery little buggers they were—he'd had the devil of a time . . .

He snapped his eyes shut, his thin, bloodless lips fluttering ever more swiftly in prayer.

Why could we not've been born pure spirits? he wondered, for perhaps the thousandth time.

The second turd plopped in the water. Always the same, always only two, no more, no less. And as always, even as a boy when he first learned to wipe his bottom all by himself, only two sheets of toilet paper, a parsimony his beaming mother was always proud of.

Pulling the chain, for this was a very old commode, then pulling up his shorts and snapping the flap shut, he moved over to the antique wash basin that was ample enough to bathe a good-sized child in, and turned on the tall hot-water tap with its white ceramic spigot, so thick it filled his hand. "They don't make them like this anymore," smiled The Cardinal, as always taking pleasure in the feel of the hard smoothness of the ancient faucet.

He washed his hands with the rose-scented soap he always preferred—"Mother of the Rose, Our Lady of the Roses," he whispered. He saw no need to go the extremes of scourging oneself, using that coarse brown lye soap—"penitential soap," he scoffingly called it—like a few he could name. He dried his hands on the Irish linen hand-towel so carefully ironed and folded by the Widow

4

Rafferty, the head housekeeper and cook below stairs, that hung fresh each morning on the rack beside the sink.

He prepared for shaving, using the same shaving mug and brush and straight razor his father had used up to the very dawn he'd dropped dead of a massive coronary, just as he was putting on his cap to go out the door to haul, as he had been hauling since he was fifteen, heavy sacks of everything imaginable on the Boston waterfront. When—55 years ago, was it?—the fuzz on his own cheeks had begun to sprout, the future Cardinal's mother presented him with the cup and brush and razor, including the well-worn strop (it'd done double duty to keep the older sons in line)—"as a keepsake of yer dear departed fawtherrr." The Cardinal had been using his dad's shaving apparatus every blessed morning ever since.

He lathered up, stropped the razor briskly, and began to shave, as always, starting at the Adam's apple, the trickiest part. Never once deviating from the way he went about it, he liked shaving; he usually got some of his best ideas for the next Sunday's homily as he scraped away.

But this dawn, other more urgent thoughts kept creeping in.

He'd learned from his spies (a term he detested—it was only that acid-tongued Monsignor Malinowski who insisted upon using it, The Cardinal preferring instead to use the more palatable "God's eyes," which he had thought up himself) that a protest demonstration was planned for later that very morning during the high mass The Cardinal himself would be saying, by that infernal group of The Disordered (The Cardinal could not bring himself to use the word "gay," seeing nothing *gay* about them) known as ACT UP, or, as it had been translated for him by

5

Brother Francis, AIDS Coalition to Unleash Power.

The Cardinal harumphed at the very idea.

His "God's eyes" had also made him aware that there would be several other "lunatic fringe" groups, as these informants termed them, joining with ACT UP, including WHAM! or, as Brother Francis again explained it, Women's Health Action and Mobilization!; plus that militant band of other pro-abortionist women called Females Against Phallocracy, or FAP—"A more screaming band of banshees never there was," sighed The Cardinal, who was familiar with their actions; and two new groups—one called WHEN, or Women's Health Education Network, and another called SNIP, or Sisters Network Invalidating Patriarchy, groups hinting—God help us, sighed The Cardinal, rolling his eyes to the vaulted ceiling—at castration in one of their flyers.

The very thought of these groups was always enough to lift The Cardinal's blood pressure several notches and, seeing in the tarnished mirror of the ancient oak medicine chest that he was scraping away rather too agitatedly and that he might very well slash his own throat if not careful, he mumbled a swift *Pater Noster* to cool his dander.

His information, as always, was impeccable. How clever it had been of him—although, as always, in order to leave no fingerprints, he had been far removed from the chain of command down through the ranks that had brought it about—to have thought of infiltrating—à la the FBI—such groups as ACT UP, with those wayward clergy whose drinking, drugging and/or sexual hankypanky (they usually went hand in hand, he found) he had gotten wind of from some of his *other* informants. One by one he had called these apostates on the carpet—the rather luxurious thick-pile carpet in the massive "parlor" of The Chancellory—and given them the ultimatum: either do penance as The Cardinal commanded or The Cardinal personally would put a flea in The Pope's ear, thus quashing all climbs up the hierarchical ladder. "Penance" meant, in light of several of the more heinous sins committed by this wayward lot, dressing in "civvies" and becoming active members of groups like ACT UP, then dutifully reporting anything and everything, especially that which even hinted of the remotest menace to the Holy Mother Church, or to his own person, back immediately to His Eminence.

None who had strayed from the path declined; several, in fact, embraced such penance with unusual ardor; it seemed to most hardly any penance at all. Their membership dues to such groups, of course, were paid out of The Cardinal's personal petty cash fund that he kept in a tightly padlocked strongbox under his canopied four-poster in his sumptuous bed chamber.

Finished shaving up his throat, The Cardinal began scraping the razor down his right cheek—always the right cheek first—careful not to cut so much as a millimeter from the somewhat longish sideburns he'd been wearing for as long a time as his pompadour.

"They'll be out in force this morning," he muttered aloud, rinsing his razor under the tap. "And there's no pleasing that bunch. I'd like to exorcise the homo out of the lot of them!" His eyes lit up at the thought. "I must speak to me Boss about *that* possibility."

Wielding his razor, he began shaving up his right cheek.

7

And those other, those unnatural, screeching harridans, those poor excuses for women, who called themselves "Pro-Choicers," The Cardinal thought grimly, his blood pressure inching up once more. And so-called Catholic women screaming right along with them, too!

He was suddenly struck with one of his shaving brainstorms: Can an unborn fetus be baptized *in vivo?*

Interesting theological fine point there, thought The Cardinal. Perhaps some of his priests at the Operation Rescue crusades, while blocking with their bodies the entrances to those abominable abattoirs called abortion clinics, could at least baptise those poor about-to-be-slaughtered lambs of God as they passed by in the bellies of those poor, benighted pregnant women, even to the forcible laying on of hands, if need be.

Yes, yes, he would send that, divinely instigated he was sure, inspiration along to the troops at the front, those militant priests—"God's terrorists," as he liked to think of them (O! how he would, by God, love to join them!)—who were the foot soldiers, the saboteurs, in the Almighty's battle against the mortal sin of baby murder.

The Cardinal was suddenly forced to clutch the edge of the massive sink at the nobility of the thought, he, *he,* "the father of thousands . . ."

Hoisting his proboscis with one stiff finger, preparatory to thinning a few of the longer hairs out of his mustache, a mustache he had begun to sport not long after he could first shave, to hide the slight hare lip he was always so touchy about, he recalled what he'd learned through his "God's eyes" of the wisecrack Monsignor Malinowski had been overheard to make to the effect that The Cardinal "lived in Medieval times in the 20th century"—Well, His Excellency saw nothing wrong with that. If the monsignor would touch base there more often, he might be a better Shepherd of God instead of standing around at diocesan cocktail parties with his smirks and his wise-cracks.

In the mirror, he tossed an impatient glance over his shoulder at the closed toilet door. Where was Brother Francis with his morning tea?

He sliced around his nose with extremely careful strokes, since, as The Cardinal himself was the first to admit, and as his older brothers and school-mates had never let him forget, he had a rather prominent honker.

But with all his preoccupations focusing on the demonstration that morning, he couldn't get The Disordered off his brain, and all this contemplation brought up that *other* cardinal (*very* lower case "c," if you please).

Fanny they called him! His thin lips pursed in contempt. Having a proclivity for fondling that certain part of the male—the very *youthful* male—anatomy. And, on top of that, that muck-raking writer daring to suggest this "Fanny" didn't even believe in God!

He swiftly crossed himself and lifted his eyes to the dark oak of the toilet's vaulted ceiling. Even so, a swifter image, as meticulously crisp as his pompadour, leapt cloven-hoofed into his mind's eye, of one of the rumors—and they were countless—of his illustrious predecessor being discovered on his knees by that Monsignor Malinowski, wouldn't you know, before "a pretty-eyed" altar boy not a half hour before high mass behind the very altar itself, and kneeling *not* in prayer.

The Cardinal blushed as red as his Christmas cope and rudely shoved the offending image from his mind as quickly as it had arisen. He was sure cardinal "Fanny" was burning in the fires of eternal damnation, if the rumors were true. Surely it could not be otherwise, so many had come forward, and his sources—his "God's eyes"—that earlier-mentioned band of troublesome priests—not to mention the odd nun or two—were unimpeachable.

The thought of the latter reminded him of that horrid little book that had appeared a few years back alleging there were nuns who were lesbians! The Cardinal's hand shook so at the thought he nicked his chin and had to apply the styptic pencil immediately, praying the cut would not show when later that morning he went, as he knew he would, before the TV cameras to denounce the demonstrators.

Alas, he sighed, as that other poor eternally damned soul, the Marquis de Sade, had said—he made a rapid sign of the cross at mention of *his* name—Evil is easy; it's the Good that's so difficult.

Where was Brother Francis? . . . Sometimes The Cardinal thought he maliciously dawdled, just to put him in a bad mood.

With an impatient tug, he tinkled the little gold bell suspended beside the oaken mirror, then rinsed his face and dried it on another neatly ironed linen hand towel that had been provided by Mrs. Rafferty. After, he briskly slapped on Old Spice—another holdover from his first days of shaving; all the boys at Immaculate Conception had used Old Spice religiously—then he dropped his shorts and, first testing the temperature with one finger, hoisted a leg over the tub and slid his lanky body down into the luxuriatingly warm water.

He dreamily closed his eyes. He was not an extremist, like the nuns in his day who took their baths wrapped from neck to ankle in voluminous flannel nightgowns so as to discourage impure thoughts and not to divert them from their contemplation on their pure and perfect marriage to Jesus Christ—although he had, in his earlier days in the seminary, as did a few of the other high-minded novitiates, in a passionate devotion to bodily purity, worn his underwear in his bath. But after a month or so he had reluctantly given it up as being too awkward and impractical. Plus the fact he was developing body sores from so much watery chafing.

Even so, now he modestly averted his eyes as his long length floated down into the water, leaving still over a yard to spare beyond his feet to the end of the tub. He curled and uncurled his toes deliciously in the invitingly pleasant warmth. But this was, as always, the only sensuous pleasure he allowed himself; he was suddenly all business, soaping up, with another bar of the rose-scented soap, a washcloth deliberately selected for its coarseness—The Cardinal believed a little scourging, at least once a day, never hurt anyone—and taking a quick, modest bath, as he had been instructed to take in the seminary and as he had been doing unchangingly for years now, permitting himself no more than two minutes all told, he rose, dripping, folded himself into the enormous clerical-black bath towel which Mrs. Rafferty had, as always, left hanging by the tub and, stepping out onto the mat, began to towel off as briskly as he had bathed.

Briskly, that is, until he reached *down there*, where he not so much rubbed as, ever more hurriedly, ever more daintily, blotted himself—*Down there*, for all its shrunk and pendant age was, from the warm bath, glowing as roseate as his Cardinal's cap, even though the unbidden stirrings of years past—which he'd always mightily

11

conquered through sweatingly mighty prayer—
had mercifully, thanks be to God, grown feebler
and feebler with age.

On the little dressing table in the corner, Mrs.
Rafferty had neatly laid out, as she did every
morning, a clean set of his underwear. The Cardinal pulled over his head the white ribbed-cotton
undershirt with the straps, the same style he'd
been wearing since high school, and snapped on
the fresh pair of clerical-black boxer shorts; then,
leaning against the table—panting a little, since
at his age even dressing was an exertion now—he
pulled on the long black rayon socks—actually
support hose masquerading as socks, for his var-
icose veins—attached the black garters—You'd
have the devil of a time finding *those* these days!
thank God for Reedy & Sons, the old Catholic-
owned haberdashery in one of the crookedly narrow lanes near the Wall Street area, where Mrs.
Rafferty, who knew all his precise measurements,
purchased his clerical garments—and slipped
into a pair of simple but expensive black Oxfords,
also purchased at Reedy & Sons, which had been
polished to mirror-brightness by Brother Francis, who had picked up the shoes outside The Cardinal's bedroom door, as he did every morning
just before dawn, while His Excellency slept.

The Cardinal then opened the age-stained mir-
rored oak door of the medicine chest and taking
out a bottle of Wildroot Cream Oil—it was a nui-
sance having to have Brother Francis order it special at the drug store on Lexington Avenue, since
it was no longer as popular as when he was a lad;
it was now even called "Wildroot Hair Groom," a
sacrilege to The Cardinal—he rubbed a generous
dollop into his scalp, especially into the lank of
hair hanging down in front, humming to himself
all the while:

12

"You better get Wildroot Cream Oil, Charlie!
Start using it today!"

as he did each morning at this moment in his
ablutions, still remembering the radio jingle after
all these years, the heavily perfumed scent of the
Wildroot's beeswax odor (the beeswax that kept
his pompadour erect) reminding him, as always,
of the scent of the beeswax candles on all of the
altars of all the churches he'd ever served in, from
parish priest starting in Altoona, PA (talk about
the boonies!), right up to, glory be to God, The Cathedral itself.

With the same wooden back hairbrush of his father's, that his mother had also given him on that
first morning of his shaving, he carefully
brushed the coxcomb of iron-gray hair up into a
stiff and sturdy "pompadour," the term used by
all the boys in his class at Immaculate Conception
(Home of The Pirates) High School for Boys in
South Boston, in the 1940s. To really shape and
style his pompadour he used, as he did then, a
wide comb, applying, as always, so much Wildroot, white greasy streaks of it showed in the rak-
ings of the comb marks. He thought he may be
old-fashioned but he couldn't give up the coiffure
of his adolescence; and he still believed, as had a
number of the shorter boys in his high school
class, that the meticulously whipped up hair
made him look several inches taller. He smiled at
himself, pulling himself up in the mirror, looking, he thought, almost six foot four at the very
least, then checked his teeth.

He clucked aloud.

He thought his choppers had appeared a bit yellow, like kernals on the cob, on the TV news the

13

other night, when he was patiently, calmly—Mrs. Rafferty had said, "With the patience of a *saint!*"—trying to explain the Church's position on abortion for the umpteenth time to the chirpy, bright-eyed TV news interviewer, an aggressive young thing if ever there was one—What was her name? Cokie? Tappie? Hickey? Perkie? One of those female TV news monickers. And her with an Irish surname too! Weren't children named after the saints anymore? He grimaced in the mirror, stretching his mouth wide with his fingers. Yes, just like kernels of corn. Have to investigate that dentist's ad he'd seen on the TV— Claimed to make your pearlies sparkling white after one application, like shoe whitener. Probably a lot of bosh. Still and all, he might give it a try . . . for the sake of his public appearance . . . As with everything these days, even religion, it paid to advertise, and it paid to look your best. The Cardinal had come to learn, as had all master manipulators of the TV, including his Boss, including his dear friend The Mayor, that image is all.

The blood rose to his cheeks, as it always did whenever he thought of it, that some, particularly that tart-tongued creature Monsignor Malinowski, said he, The Cardinal, "could sniff out a TV camera within a fifty-block radius of The Cathedral"; worse yet, he had also spread the rumor that The Cardinal had gotten his red hat solely by "kissing The Pope's ass" (the monsignor was not above crudities), and by swearing on a stack of Papal Bulls he'd make American Catholics "toe the line."

Monsignor Malinowski, thought The Cardinal, darkly. Except for The Disordered and the Pro-Choicers, nothing got his dander up as much as that one. Had the monsignor been a thorn in The

14

Crown of Christ you could be sure it would've been the sharpest thorn. The Cardinal suspected the monsignor of daily honing his tongue on a razor strop.

Preparatory to putting it away, he gave his own straight razor a few vigorous strops.

"'Ambition is the lust of the clergy,'" he mimicked, mimicking in his head the musical voice, that always set his teeth on edge, of Monsignor Malinowski, who'd probably stolen the quote from someone, as The Cardinal suspected he did all his allegedly "witty " remarks. And another thing, His Excellency had strong doubts about the monsignor, what with the flutey voice, the fluttery hands—suspecting him also to be "one of them," one of The Disordered.

"If, by God, I ever find proof," he growled, washing the last of the lather out of his shaving brush, then inspecting the bloody razor nick on his chin (he best put some No. 2 pancake makeup on that; it might show up on the TV), "I'll ship him off to a diocese in the boonies so fast his collar'll spin."

The Cardinal's "God's eyes," of course, were still diligently pursuing the matter, a fact Monsignor Malinowski was well aware of, which made his barbs in front of The Cardinal's minions all the sharper, since he knew that they would get back within half an hour of their first utterance to His Eminence's ears and, knowing his intended victim to a faretheewell, send his blood pressure skyhigh.

That, of course, was just one more reason why the monsignor was never ever invited to that signal honor: the vesting ceremony of The Cardinal in the sacristy for the high mass that The Cardinal celebrated each Sunday on The Cathedral altar, just as he would be in a few short hours.

Nor, as far as The Cardinal was concerned,

would the monsignor ever be invited to view that ceremony until he put a leash on his tongue.

He preferred to see the monsignor's bile as sour grapes for *his* not getting the red hat that now sat on The Cardinal's own brilliantined head.

Fearing his thoughts were bordering on the maliciously unChristian, The Cardinal said a hasty prayer for the soul, not to mention the sharp tongue, of the monsignor, as he put his shaving equipment back into the huge antique medicine chest.

His black silken cassock with its red piping, freshly sponged and neatly pressed with a luke-warm iron that very morning by Mrs. Rafferty, hung on the back of the toilet door on a velvet-lined hanger, as it always did, after Brother Francis delivered it from downstairs each morning. The Cardinal slipped into it, then again pulled impatiently at the little gold bell beside the mirror. After a few long moments, the door of the bath swished open and plump, middle-aged Brother Francis darted in with, as always, noted The Cardinal, frowning, his plump left thumb stuck in The Cardinal's no longer steaming mug of morning tea. In his coarse, brown, monk's cloth robe, knotted at the middle with a belt of the rosary with beads as big as pingpong balls—a bit ostentatious, The Cardinal always thought—from which hung a heavy leaden-hued crucifix, Brother Francis set the mug on the edge of the massive sink, then with a hurried "Good morning, your grace," went down on his knees, as The Cardinal turned to have his cassock buttoned from the floor up. While the Brother's fat but nimble fingers were thus occupied, The Cardinal, as he did every single blessed morning, looked down on Brother Francis with distaste, seeing the perennial red scales of psoriasis even through the tonsured strawberry-blonde hair at the top of his pate.

He picked up the mug of Mrs. Rafferty's tea and, as he also did every morning, suspiciously eyed its dark-as-mud surface. Brother Francis's "misfortune" extended to the backs of his hands and, as he invariably did, The Cardinal muttered to himself, envisioning flakes of psoriatic skin snowing into his tea from the offending thumb. Ointments, unguents, endless dermatologists, coupled with endless prayer, were all to no avail. The Cardinal wondered if it was some sickness in the Brother's soul leaking through his skin (he always had a sneaking suspicion about the good Brother's extreme unctuousness), because The Cardinal believed all such eruptions were rooted in this, from the pimples of adolescence (cause: self-pollution, a wasting of the seed if ever there was one) to skin cancer (cause: a disordered faith that invades the very cells themselves) to the lesions of Kaposi's Sarcoma in those with AIDS (cause: *contra naturam* practices and more abominable wasting of the seed), all Divine Punishments from on high.

The Cardinal felt somewhat uneasy that these attitudes just *might* be taken as unChristian and, particularly in the case of Brother Francis, he prayed daily to be relieved of them. When he wasn't, he pretended to be Saint Francis, embracing and swooning in the arms of the scrofulous; in fact, the opportunity to repeat this little drama on a daily basis was one of the chief reasons he kept Brother Francis on his personal staff—"It keeps me humble," he breathed piously, and truly believed it.

Unfortunately, this pietistic sentiment lasted

17

only until he noted Brother Francis's thumb stuck in his tea mug on the next morning around.

Even though it annoyed him, even frightened him more than a little, afraid it might be catching—and wouldn't that be a nice sight for the TV cameras, a Prince of the Church with blotches on his face to match the color of his cap!—he'd become resigned to it, had had to, since, even though he'd spoken to Brother Francis countless times about his dunking his thumb in his teacup, even trying a little lighthearted humor at first, saying Francis's thumb was "no cruller, ha-ha," it had been a waste of time.

Saint Francis himself could have done no more, he sighed to himself, as The Saint's namesake smartly buttoned the thirtieth and final button and The Cardinal gingerly placed his hand on the Brother's scabrous head and murmured his daily but cursory blessing. Then, leaving Brother Francis to clean up, he plucked a freshly-laundered red skull cap from its peg on the back of the bathroom door, lowered it ever so reverently on the back of his head so as not to disarrange a hair of his immaculately oiled pompadour and, ready for whatever God gave him this day, strode out of the bath.

Even though The Cardinal had a great deal of beforehand information on what lay before him on that particular morning, thanks to his "God's eyes" and The Mayor's secret police, had he even the slightest inkling of the plans a certain trio, who were squatters in an abandoned tenement down on Avenue D, had for him that day, he might very well not have ventured out of the relative sanctuary of The Chancellory.

One very good reason for this was The Poet, already introduced as Peter, who wanted to kill The Cardinal.

At the very moment The Cardinal was departing his toilet in The Chancellory, the skinny, underfed frame of The Poet was slouched over his rickety writing table (found in a trash heap over on 2nd Avenue), as he scratched away at trying to write a poem on a piece of scrap paper in his tiny two-room apartment down in the depths of the Lower East Side's Alphabet City:

How fragrant are the nuts of men in May

he scribbled.

Then, as often happened, realizing he was mistaking horniness, no doubt generated by the warmth of spring, for poetic inspiration—aside from The Cardinal, sex was his other obsession— he balled up the paper and tossed it over his shoulder.

"In patriarchy," thought The Poet, in another moment of inspiration, "Pen is penis." In spite of that, he liked to think he "wrote with his penis," just as Renoir said he'd painted with his.

So, next he scribbled:

> *pen is*
> *penis*

Then added, for parity, for, as a post-patriarchal poet, he was nothing if not androgynous:

> *also*
> *clitor is*

But The Poet was so jumpy, he couldn't concentrate. He'd only been trying to write a poem all night—the few moments of sleep he'd been able to snatch had been filled with nightmarish terror—to take his mind off what he would be doing later that morning. (*"How do I hate thee—Let me count the ways,"* had been, bearing The Cardinal in mind, another of his aborted attempts.)

Leaping out of his wobbly writing chair (carried boldly out of a flea market on 6th Avenue in Chelsea one Sunday afternoon), he once more paced the squeaky, loose boards of his squatter's flat.

He had never assassinated anyone before.

Through the open windows, he swore he caught the green scent of early budding trees wafting over the lettered blocks of Alphabet City from Tompkins Square, while from below, out on Avenue D, a loud olio of Latino music blasted into the room from the tape decks in the double-parked cars and gypsy cabs being repaired at curbside from early morning til late into the night, in all seasons, by the gypsy mechanics, many of them, like the car owners themselves, from the Dominican Republic, operating out of an abandoned store front in the building next door. FLAT FIX read a sandwich board sign in crudely painted letters at the curb.

The music was getting on his nerves. Everything was getting on his nerves. He felt feverish; he found himself wondering what kind of underwear The Cardinal wore; boxer shorts, probably, like his own father, or maybe underdrawers that looked like they were made in 1912? . . . He wished it were afternoon and the whole thing over with and himself locked up in The Tombs, as he was certain he would be.

The Cardinal was all he could think about. Not that he knew The Cardinal personally, of course, although, over time, he had come to feel he did:

Not only did The Poet listen to all the put downs of The Cardinal's policies on the gay and lesbian programs on WBAI-FM on the SONY Walkman that had somehow one morning found its way into his knapsack during a visit to an electronics store over on 7th Avenue, but he also watched every one of The Cardinal's TV appearances, which seemed even more numerous than those of the particular celebrity of the moment, watched them on the tiny, blurry screen of his black and white Motorola portable TV set—another of his "found objects," this time in a trash can over on Avenue A (with a little fiddling, Tom The Trickster from downstairs had gotten it working again)—and read every word uttered by The Cardinal and dutifully printed by *The New York Times* (daily free copies of which The Poet snatched on the run from various newsstands around the neighborhood, feigning to be a Yuppie jogger from the gentrified housing around Tompkins Square, and racing by so fast in his gray Champions, the news-dealers barely glimpsed him (he hadn't been on the track team in high school *only* to be with the boys in the shower room), but he also had been having long theological and ethical arguments with The Cardinal in his own head, where The Cardinal had been living for some time now, rent free—just as The Poet was also living rent free, compliments of his "landlord," The City of New York, which owned the abandoned building he and Tom The Trickster and Deirdre The Rad Dyke and Asmaralda were squatters in.

All of this was thanks to Tom The Trickster, the "tenant" a few floors below The Poet, who had first discovered the place and broken into it a year ago, the slightly older Tom, former Wall Street wizard and now rabid gay activist, who had taught The Poet his street smarts. (He had also ingeniously rigged up a line from the lamp post in front of the house so it would take very sharp Con Ed eyes indeed to detect it, thus providing free juice for all his squatter friends.)

But The Cardinal, ah, The Cardinal . . . The Poet saw him as a devoted man, but he also saw that devotion to ignorance is no virtue.

"Thousands of people we love are dying," he thought, bitterly. He saw The Cardinal's actions as "contributing to those deaths . . ."

"If 'evil is the inability to imagine the lives of others,'" thought The Poet aloud as he continued to pace the floor, paraphrasing Eli Wiesel's words about those who gave the world the Nazi death camps, "then The Cardinal, including The Pope, is one of the most evil men on earth."

The Poet believed he would really be doing humanity a favor by ridding it of such an unimaginative excrescence—a moral act.

He snatched a fresh piece of scrap paper from the huge pile on the floor and hurriedly penned with his 17¢ BIC pen:

> *If only*
> *The Cardinal's*
> *old man'd*
> *worn*
> *a rubber*
> *that night*

Having no knowledge, of course, that The Cardinal's Sainted Mother would never, never have permitted such a thing in her house, at first, he crumpled this one up too, but then thought better of it. Smoothing out the paper as best he could, he slipped it under an Empire State Building paperweight that was holding down a very slim pile of "acceptable" poems (as to be expected, most of them dealt with either sex or The Cardinal), slim in contrast to the mountain of balled up paper of months and months of rejects rearing up behind his wobbly folding chair.

He would, as he often did with his few "better" poems, try this one out on Tom The Trickster.

Not that he knew when he'd get the chance to read it to him, since Tom hadn't let anyone, not even Peter The Poet, into his flat for days now. Peter wondered what new trick he was going to come up with for The Demo, the ACT UP and WHAM! signs for which had been plastered all over Chelsea and the West and East Village for weeks now. STOP THE CHURCH, they were all headlined, and gave information for the place—The Cathedral on 5th Avenue—and the date and time—that very morning at 9:30 a.m. They announced a call to protest the Church's, and more specifically, The Cardinal's, position on AIDS, abortion, and homosexuality.

But rather than write about The Cardinal, The Poet, nervous wreck that it made him, at this point really only wanted to blow The Cardinal's brains out with the aforementioned semi-automatic he'd been hiding away on the top shelf of the roach-infested cabinet in his hole-in-the-wall kitchen for weeks now. He was fired with the belief that if The Cardinal (not to mention The Pope, any Pope) burned in Hell for two thousand years, it would not atone for the inhumane horrors—the murderous contempt for women, the equally murderous homophobia, just to cite two examples on The Poet's long list of grudges—The Cardinal helped inflict deliberately upon humanity.

"All that Papal Bull shit," he snorted.

He was firmly convinced that shooting The Cardinal would somehow end the persecution not only of gay and lesbian people in the city but of women as well, not yet having the years to know, as with The Pope, there would always be another one.

Even if he were still wet behind the ears in some respects, The Poet, à la Whitman, was very much aware of his contradictions, and that to be human was to be full of contradictions. It was, after all, all about being human, wasn't it? To try to be coherent was, to him, banal; that is, "trying to reconcile opposites wasn't the point but to be endlessly fascinated by the surprises and revelations they offered"—and, of course, to write poems about them.

He saw the act of writing as a sacred act.

Grabbing another sheet of scrap paper from the pile, he scribbled afresh:

> A .38 magnum bullet
> baring
> your heart
> like
> the "Sacred" Heart
> of your Jesus

That "sacred" snippet ended up, too, on the reject pile.

No, he could not sit still. He could not write on such a morning. He glanced yet again at his Timex watch, a gift from Tom The Trickster who said he'd "found" it in a drug store on Avenue C.

6:30 a.m.

The Poet leapt from his chair and began pacing again.

There were now at least a half dozen different Latino beats throbbing up from the street. He clapped his hands against his ears. Even with that, even, as he well knew, with the windows closed, he could still hear that insistent beat. Figuring if you can't fight 'em, join 'em, he started dancing around, undulating his hips and snapping his fingers, but it just wasn't there—his obsession with The Cardinal and what he was about to do to him had driven out even his ability to dance.

Before he'd left his family's split-level house in suburban Pearl River, New York, and moved to this squalid little apartment in Alphabet City to pursue his "calling," as he called it, to be "the biggest, baddest faggot poet in all Manahatta," he had rather liked Latino music, especially merengue and salsa. In fact, he had even wiggled his naked hips to it as a teenager, as it throbbed through his stereo in the privacy of his bedroom (his two older brothers, with whom he had shared the room, were then off to Saint Sebastian-of-the-Arrows College in upstate New York), a pristine-painted bedroom, its walls covered with pictures of Jesus and Mary and any number of saints, including a Mother-of-Pearl rosary blessed by The Pope himself, hanging above his bed. How guilty he'd felt at first dancing nude with all those saintly eyes peering down on him, but he solved that by covering the pictures (including the Pope-blessed rosary) with tissues. "You sure go through more boxes of Kleenex than all of us put together," his mother had complained; and it was true, for he also used that handy pull-out box when, having reached that ecstatic intensity in his solo dancing where he could no longer contain himself (the beige DuPont nylon wall-to-wall was guaranteed stain-proof but he still didn't want to risk leaving any tell-tale clues for his sharp-eyed mother), he caught the sap of his adolescent happiness in wad after wad of it, which he

25

stealthily flushed down the toilet afterwards, a toilet, he always said, kept so sparklingly scrubbed by his mother, you could drink out of it.

Since leaving Pearl River, he called home once a month, collect, of course, to let his mother know he was still alive (he never told her *where* he was living, however). Their conversations always went something like this: She said, "I'm still saying a rosary for you everyday." He said, "Stop wasting your time on medieval gibberish." She said, "Where did I go wrong?" He said, "It's the rightest thing you ever did in your life." Click.

His father, of course, never wanted to speak to him, ever, once he'd learned his youngest son "liked kissing men on the mouth."

So now he was a "fallen Catholic," but one who, in falling, had miraculously discovered his fairy wings.

He'd been flying ever since.

But now, after months of it, morning, noon, and night, he had come to detest "cha-cha" music, as he now sneeringly called it. This in spite of his occasionally hanging out in the Nuyorican Poets' Cafe over on East 3rd between Avenues B and C where Loisaida played and where Latina and Latino poets of Alphabet City read their work; even though he understood only a few words of Spanish from Spanish 101 at Pearl River High, still, he loved the gritty, passionate music, the fiery rhythms of their poems.

However, the music clamoring in his windows had by now burrowed into his middle ear, the beats beating out his own rhythms, not to mention his minimal ability to concentrate. "Cha-cha" was really getting on his nerves, almost as much as his skittishness about blowing away The Cardinal.

As he did as a kid in his suburban backyard

through a pile of autumn leaves, he now angrily kicked his way through the heap of balled up poems, his "dead leaves of grass," as he rather dramatically termed them, cockroaches scattering in all directions, and went to one of the windows, where the panes were so gray with grime— The Poet thought the years of accumulated soot lent a poetically drear atmosphere to his "atelier," as he affectedly called it—it *was*, after all, under the roof—grime that also lent a kind of underground now-I-see-in-darkness sort of dimness, à la "Edgar Allan Mole," as he affectionately nicknamed the poet, the right purblind light for any poet to write in, he believed—and so, since he never washed them, he could barely see out of them. But at least he *had* windows: those on the first floor where Tom The Trickster preferred to live The City had walled up with cinderblocks.

> "You be better bein' a maggot
> than a sicko faggot,"

thumped up from one of the tape decks below, rapping on his windows with an insistent beat, as similar rap lyrics did day after day.

> "Foreigners, and faggots
> knocking down my nation . . ."

blared up from a gypsy cab's stereo system, owned no doubt by one of those very same "foreigners."

To let off steam more than anything else, he leaned out the window as far as he could into the cacaphony of rap and salsa roaring up from below and, fond of old Neapolitan airs (he wasn't a faggot for nothing), he piped his own idiosyncratic version of one at the top of his lungs, "O

SODOMIO! O SODOMIO!" while the Latino mechanics below, in their greasy sock hats and coveralls, gave him the finger, serenading back up to him, "O MARICŌN-A! O MARICŌN-A!"

The Poet was not unknown on the streets, particularly on *that* block.

He flung down the rattly window, splinters flying everywhere from the rotting frames. At that moment, he didn't know who he wanted to murder more: The Cardinal or the gypsy auto mechanics. And as for their taunts, he sneered, well, if they had to live for even a day in the skin of an American faggot, they'd know what *cojones* really were.

Suddenly he was very hungry. This surprised him enormously. He'd heard somewhere that murderers, after they'd done the deed, ate like pigs; and here he was, the job not even begun yet and he was suddenly ravenous.

"Nervous belly," he thought.

He went into the dark hole of a kitchen and flung open the sagging cabinet doors above the foul-smelling sink piled high with dirty dishes—all that he owned, a variety of cracked and ill-assorted plates and cups he'd slipped, unwashed, into his knapsack from several greasy spoons in the neighborhood. He inspected the interior of the cupboard: Nothing but the usual zillion cockroaches darting everywhere—he wondered what they lived on in *his* apartment. There was a half-filled jar of stale instant coffee pinched from the local Red Apple supermarket—where he preferred to "shop," in his army overcoat with its capacious inner pockets he'd sewn in specially—at Tom's suggestion—and a few packets of soup crackers he'd filched from the greasy spoon on Avenue B the other day when Tom The Trickster, having fallen into a few coins, had treated him to a bowl of hearty lentil soup.

He saw from the bareness of his cupboard he would have to go "shopping" again very soon, then laughed at the thought. By nightfall, he'd undoubtedly be cooling his heels in solitary, booked for murder. The thought of it made him so suddenly dizzy, he gripped the edge of the sink, just as his intended victim had done earlier that dawn, but for a different reason, in the toilet of The Chancellory.

The Tombs would be taking care of his three squares a day from now on.

He held his Timex up to the weak light from the narrow airshaft window. 7 a.m. He'd leave for The Cathedral in another hour. He knew once he got going, he'd calm down a bit.

Ripping open the wrappers, he chomped hungrily on the crackers, washing them down with a dipperful of water from the bucket beside the sink (Tom The Trickster, for all his trickery, hadn't yet figured out how to get the water turned back on—actually, most of the pipes had been stolen long before by junkies—so all four inhabitants of the abandoned tenement had to collect their water from a fire hydrant at the street corner that Tom—with his handy firefighter's wrench, stolen off one of the neighborhood fire company's trucks while a blaze was fought in yet another of the abandoned City-owned tenements down the block—made run all year round at a modest trickle—he was also a conservationist—a feat that put him in favor not only with the three others he'd invited in to share the place, but with the junkies who squatted in the other empty buildings along the street, not to mention the car and livery owners below who were able to wash their autos while waiting in line for repairs. The Poet daily lugged his water up the four flights from the hydrant in several battered buckets he'd found in the basement of the building when he and Tom first went scavenging down there, hauling water, as well, for Asmaralda, who lived in the apartment behind him, and for Deirdre The Rad Dyke, who lived directly below him.

As for washing up and taking care of "biological functions," as his mother euphemistically called them, those he satisfied at a restroom in a cut-rate gas station down the block, where the young and attractively curly-haired Puerto Rican attendant, for the occasional hand job, let him use the facilities, which really weren't any cleaner than his own sink, whenever he wished.

Hence, because bathing was no longer a top priority with him, The Poet always had a bit of an odor about him—he preferred to think of it as "an animal odor," the proper smell for a poet worthy of the name, agreeing with D. H. Lawrence who said something to the effect that too much bathing impoverishes the blood.

This, of course, from a boy who came from a home where not to shower at least once a day wasn't exactly a mortal sin, but close to it. One can only imagine what his mother and father would have thought, had they known. But of course they didn't know, and that was the way he preferred it. As for his own stench and the stench of humanity (The Poet did get off on body smells, particularly male body smells), he agreed with Tacitus: "*Nihil humanum mihi alienum est*" ("Nothing human is foreign to me").

Before he shut the cabinet doors, he reached up to the top shelf, just as he did every morning, and felt for the gun. It gave him comfort knowing it was there. He took it down very gingerly, still shy with it and nervous that it might suddenly go off (he would've unloaded it but couldn't figure out how and was equally concerned he might not be able to reload it). He worried what it would sound and feel like at the crucial moment, a moment that was now fast approaching: Would it leap out of his hand like a live fish, spoiling his aim? Would its firing deafen him? Besides his fear of it, he hadn't practiced firing the pistol for two reasons: (a.) Where did you practice shooting a gun on the Lower East Side? (The bullets zinging around Alphabet City were not shot for the practice.) And, (b.), he didn't want to waste any of the bullets in the fully-loaded chamber, just in case he shot wildly the first couple of tries, or The Cardinal turned out to be spryer at ducking than he anticipated.

Going to the windows in the front room he held it, as he had dozens of times already, up to the dreary light. Far less sophisticated than some of the weapons the drug dealers toted around in the streets below, it was an official New York City Police Department 9 millimeter semi-automatic that he'd accidentally stumbled on in its shoulder holster while his arms passionately encircled the upper torso of a tipsy off-duty detective he was kneeling before on one of the piers along West Street one hot August night last summer. (The Poet, being an expert and quite artful cocksucker, was known, among those who knew him intimately, as "The Head Master.") As the cop began groaning and convulsing, "shooting his blanks in the air," as The Poet put it, practicing one of *his* versions of "safer sex," the scent of semen whizzing past his nostrils like the scent of the ailanthus (or Tree of Heaven, as he poetically preferred it) under Deirdre's windows, The Poet had stealthily slid the gun out of its harness and

31

down into the crotch of his levis, realizing at that moment, with a surge of ecstasy beyond the thrill of any blow job, that he finally had, between his legs, the weapon to carry out his long-simmering scheme.

Springing up, leaving the detective standing slack-jawed and flat-footed with his trousers down around his ankles, while across the Hudson the lights of Hoboken had twinkled between his rubbery legs, Peter The Poet, former Pearl River High School long-distance runner champ, had run lightly through the side streets of the West Village in the still-sweltering pre-dawn hours, his hand down his levis clutching the pistol, so exhilarated by this latest "found object," he didn't stop til he had arrived at the secret basement entrance at the side of the abandoned building on Avenue D.

It was not the first gun he had handled.

He had been a *curious* child—in more ways than one, as his older brothers all agreed, calling him "fairy" and "faggot" from a tender age—but he had also shown a great deal of curiosity: in short, like any budding poet, he was a great snoop and had early on discovered his father's unloaded pistol hidden away in the bottom drawer of his bedroom dresser beneath his pile of boxer shorts (that they glistened snowy white once the wife got through with them, goes without saying) and loved to sneak into the bedroom when no one was about and rifle through his father's shorts til he found the gun; then, taking it and laying it tenderly in his open palm as if it were a live thing, he liked stroking the hard metal of the barrel, so sensuously silky under his caress in its high-polished smoothness.

Even though only a budding poet, he under-

stood even then that every son is a potential father killer—and every father, because he was
once a son himself, knows it. Hence, he understood as well, the cruelty of fathers against sons,
their never turning their backs on them.

"If my pop had porked me once in a while, or
vice-versa," sighed The Poet again, in yet another
of his innumerable sighs, "we might've gotten
along a helluva lot better."

He had even penned a long opus on this penetrating insight which he entitled "Poppycock."

Blame it on his being a poet, blame it even more
on his being a Pisces, but in this matter of shooting The Cardinal, The Poet had no specific plan as
to how he would go about it (all he knew was a
citizen these days only had redress to a problem if
he or she got on TV, and thus he had his speech
planned, for afterwards, of why he did it, but that
is as far as his planning went); he didn't even
know what The Cardinal's movements would be
that morning, as Tom The Trickster knew,
thanks to the anonymous tips left once or twice a
week on ACT UP's answering machine by a honeyed voice that queerly enough sounded eerily
like The Cardinal himself, tips some in ACT UP
scoffed at as being those of a prankster or a dis-
informer; but Tom The Trickster found them
often accurate, and certainly useful for *his* plans,
anyway; Peter didn't even know that The Cardinal had bodyguards—retired Irish-Catholic cops,
including one karate instructor with a black belt,
all of them dressed in clerical drag, semi-
automatics, not unlike The Poet's stolen one, riding on their hips inside the side slits of their cas-
socks; and, of course, he had no experience shooting a gun and, hence, as already noted, was no
marksman.

33

As a result, he was the most dangerous kind of assassin possible where, as in the world of quantum mechanics, randomness achieves results.

Now he pointed the gun at the window, where, even though the sun was just rising over the housing projects roofs across the way, the ashen light pushing weakly through the grime gave the metal of the barrel a cold, sinister hardness, a hardness matching the tiny smile now curling Peter The Poet's lips.

Meanwhile, The Cardinal himself was feeling a pinch of hunger as he sniffed the delicious aromas of Mrs. Rafferty's breakfast in the air as he descended the broad, plushly carpeted curving stairs of The Chancellory, with its gray stone walls and gilded floral patterns carved in stone at the corners, and headed toward the high-ceilinged, dark-paneled dining room with its long mahogany table and snowy-white napery and sparkling silverware, set for one. Especially now that he was getting on, and although he was a stickler—or "stick in the mud," as Monsignor Malinowski put it—for tradition, he was grateful that The Pope, in his holy wisdom, had shortened the fasting time before partaking of The Host at mass to one hour—10:30 a.m. *was* a long way away.

His stomach growled just thinking of it.

And there was Mrs. Rafferty herself, her tumbling gray hair piled high on her head, and wearing an apron as white as her tablecloth, laying out His Excellency's breakfast at one end of a table that could easily seat fifty: eggs over easy, steak and kidneys cut up bite-sized by Mrs. Rafferty's own hands; thick Irish oatmeal, made only from steel-rolled oats imported specially from

Dublin, and served with heavy cream, a big dollop of sweet butter and sprinkled with nutmeg; Irish soda bread buttered already with more great chunks of sweet butter, the way The Cardinal liked it, buttered by Mrs. Rafferty herself—such a busy man, if she could save him some time, what was the harm in spoiling him a smidgeon?—and another mug of black Irish Breakfast tea steaming by his plate.

Yes, he knew he would need a hearty breakfast for the busy *and* troublesome hours ahead.

"Top a' the marnin', Mrs. R.," he smiled, mimicking his Sainted Mother's best brogue.

Mrs. Rafferty curtsied, then pulled back His Eminence's high-backed dining room chair with its intricate carvings of angels blowing trumpets and its deep velvet seat the same shade of red as The Cardinal's cap.

"Goo-o-o-o-d marnin', yer Grace," cooed Mrs. Rafferty, imitating nobody but herself.

Meanwhile, back on Avenue D, four floors below The Poet's "atelier," Tom The Trickster, wearing nothing but a jock strap, knelt on the floor of his "commandeered" apartment, as he preferred to think of it, broad paint brush in hand, putting the finishing touches to a six foot by seventy-five foot nylon banner (nylon was so light, foldable and compact, and unfurled so snappily). He'd been working on it secretly for some time now, not even giving a hint of his project to Peter The Poet, who had been snooping around, trying his damnedest to find out what he was up to.

Weighted lightly at its bottom with stones he had found in the vacant lot behind the tenement and sewn into the bottom hem to give it weight and snap when it dropped, the banner had a length of rope running through the top hem (his crude stitches looking like those in Dr. Frankenstein's Monster's forehead).

He would not have ever in his wildest dreams foreseen that he, being early on a wizard at figures who had planned his future as a multimillionaire when he was in grade school in Lima, Ohio (where he'd first begun to notice as well the figures of the boys in his class and was passionately curious as to what not a few of them looked like out of their boy-sized Wranglers), would end up broke and a squatter in a falling-down abandoned building in a rundown corner of a great city, painting banners in the nude. Even back then, when, being so clever a trickster, he'd managed to find out just what those school chums that caught his eye did look like *sans* their denims, he'd had no inkling. And he'd been successfully making money on the stock market and tricking boys out of their pants (boyish good looks and eyes that said, Only You Matter To Me In This World, helped too), up until that day, having had a dry cough for several weeks, night sweats and a general feeling of malaise, he'd finally gone to see his doctor.

The same day that Tom The Trickster was diagnosed with AIDS in his doctor's office on East 70th Street, not far from his own fashionable and very expensively furnished apartment around the corner, he took a cab back downtown to Wall Street. Before he returned to the brokerage house where he worked, he went up to the visitors gallery of The New York Stock Exchange, something he hadn't done since that day of his high school senior class trip to New York City where, in the class' visit to The Exchange, he first had his vision that he would someday be where the money

36

was, and where that was was obvious to his then young but sharply perceptive eyes.

But on the day of his diagnosis, as he stood leaning over the rail, watching the hubbub on the floor below, the wild and wild-eyed gesticulatings, the frantic hands snatching the air, the bedlam of shouts, and seeing the banks and banks of flashing green computer screens, the endless flickering electronic tapes skittering around the high walls, all of it suddenly to him like some incomprehensible vision of modern hell, he had another vision: he saw that money, truly, was shit, and that he and America were kneedeep in it.

Little did he know then that, not many weeks after, feeling poorly and debating if he should continue on in his job or not, he would be standing in that exact spot once more in The Exchange's visitors gallery, dressed in that same brokerage-dark, conservatively cut business suit, and would be startled out of his wits when a band of similarly dressed ACT UP members, sporting fake bond traders name tags, to gain entry, rushed onto the balcony. While shrilly blowing whistles and setting off marine fog horns, they began scattering queer—as in "queer-as-a-three-dollar-bill"—money, phony 100s, 50s and 10s created by the activist artists group Gran Fury, down onto the floor of The Exchange, the backs of the bills reading: FUCK YOUR PROFITEERING. PEOPLE ARE DYING WHILE YOU PLAY BUSINESS. AID$ NOW.

The brokers went nuts trying to snatch up the fake bills, more proof to Tom, once he regained his senses, of the money-driven madness of their lives, and his own, and in that instant he had a powerful third vision of an insane system he would, until his last breath, thank AIDS for rescuing him from, for, impulsively snatching a fist-ful of queer money from one of the ACT UP people, he joined the rest in showering the bills down onto the trading floor below.

That was the day he was arrested for the first time in his life, along with the others, for "crimi-nal impersonation"—or "bad stock broker drag," as some wag in ACT UP put it—a "class A misde-meanor," of which he was inordinately proud.

It would not be his last arrest, but it was his last job. Before they fired him, he quit the brokerage house and joined ACT UP to do whatever he could for whatever time he had left.

After that, there was no turning back.

It was while walking through Alphabet City several weeks after his release from jail, on his way to run errands for one of his AIDS buddies in the neighborhood, who was too sick to get out, that he'd discovered the abandoned tenement on Avenue D, and, after poking around, stumbled on its concealed entrance. Having moved from apart-ment to apartment of friends for weeks now, his funds running low, and, having lost his health coverage, doctor bills rapidly eating up his sav-ings, he figured he might be able to make the place livable.

After seeing to his buddy's needs, he returned to the building on Avenue D and, after inspecting it from top to bottom, with nothing but a flash-light and a rolled up sleeping bag, he had moved in that very same night.

Living by his wits, including hands that were swifter than any shop owner's eyes, he had been squatting there ever since.

This morning at The Cathedral, he thought, with a rush of excitement, as he stood up to better survey his touch-up job on the banner, would top not only his escapade at The Stock Exchange but all his other escapades as well.

He took a swig of "tea" from the old mayonnaise jar Asmaralda upstairs left outside his door each morning. Wary when, at first, without a word, she had started leaving the steaming jar at his door, he had snatched a stray cat off the street, brought it home and mixed the "tea" in with some milk, which the half-starved cat lapped up hungrily. When the cat, who still hung around the building and turned out to be a good mouser and ratter, sort of belonging to everybody in the house, not only survived but began to thrive (as would, subsequently, Tom himself, the more he drank of Asmaralda's brew), he felt reassured. He'd been drinking her "tea" for some time now and, in spite of his condition, his cough and night sweats gradually had disappeared and he began feeling more energy than ever, for reasons he himself could not explain, nor could his doctor, either.

He hadn't had to see his doctor for months now.

Since the windows in this apartment had all been walled up with cinderblocks by the City to keep out intruders such as himself and his friends, he dragged along beside him on a long extension cord, a bent and rusty wrought-iron floor lamp he'd rewired after he'd found it speared into the top of a can of garbage over on 2nd Avenue one night as he and Peter The Poet were returning from an ACT UP meeting at the Lesbian and Gay Community Center over on West 13th Street. The juice, of course, like all the juice in the house, was compliments of Con Ed—due, as mentioned earlier, to Tom's handiwork in shimmying up the pole outside the tenement and tapping into their line.

39

He was doing the last minute touching up of the enormous block letters with lavender paint, letters that ran the entire length of the bright red banner which he'd cleverly scissored in the shape of an enormous erect phallus, with wings, the latter sprouting airily out from the balls.

There is no need to go into all the details of how he acquired the materials necessary to create his handiwork. Since he had taken the vow of poverty, he made it a point to "appropriate" ("stealing" was such an *ugly* word) only from the more homophobic shopkeepers (which gave him a lot of latitude since many of the businesses in the neighborhood were run by males, as he termed it, "with terminal machismo") and corporate chains, like Red Apple and Ace Hardware, which were, to him, too vast and abstract to be considered owned by actual people. (After many night-long discussions, he and The Poet upstairs had concluded that everything in the USA was corporate-connected, from the corporate President in The White House to the corporate Congress and corporate Pentagon—"Pentagonorrhea," as The Poet had referred to it in one of the innumerable poems he slipped under Tom's door—to the corporate Media.)

For the record, however, the bolt of red nylon for the banner he'd hoisted out of a bin filled with used World War II parachutes in front of a discount odds and ends fabric shop owned by rabidly anti-*feygele* Orthodox Jews down on Delancey Street.

Suffice it to say, unlike The Poet on occasion, Tom did not, having taken as well a vow of celibacy, make use of his considerable fleshly charms to obtain his acquisitions, nor did he do so in order to make use of the gas station rest room at the corner for his "biological needs," laying instead the occasional toy model race car on the cute Puerto Rican gas jockey, toy cars which he "found" in a hobby shop in the West Village, after he had discovered the youth was an avid collector.

It was, as noted, Tom The Trickster who taught the relatively innocent Poet from the suburbs how to survive on the street, including the art of "appropriation"—which, it was immediately apparent to him, The Poet, like himself, had an inborn affinity for—so that Tom thought of himself as a kind of, as he put it, "youthful Fagin, or Faggin" to The Poet.

When they'd first met, at an ACT UP meeting at The Lesbian and Gay Community Center, The Poet, who had been living on the wintry streets for some days since his arrival in Manhattan and who had only wandered into The Center to get warm, had tried to impress Tom with his wit. It went something like this:

Peter: "Do you know what the masochist sings to the sadist?"

Tom: "Ya' got me."

Peter: "No, 'I Get a Kick Out of You.' Have you heard the song 'Old Fairies Never Die, They Just Blow Away'? . . ."

Tom: "No, I haven't."

Peter: "Did you ever stop to think that Alice Faye in pig latin is 'phallus'?"

Tom: "No, I never did."

Peter: "Guess what I'm pinning on my fly this Christmas."

Tom: "I give up."

Peter: "A sprig of mistletoe."

Etc., etc.

In spite of this embarrassing display of adolescent greenery, Tom The Trickster still invited Peter to squat with him on Avenue D.

Speaking of which, with his boyish good looks

and irresistably innocent boyish grin—not to mention his thoroughly attractive boyish body, which was readily apparent in the warm golden light of the lamp as he, the Master Squatter, squatted in his athletic supporter over the banner—being nude or almost nude, he felt, helped him do his best work—dabbing here, dabbing there with his brush—additional charms were also apparent in the nut-hardness of his creamy buttocks, in the dark line of fine animal-like hair cleaving those "two succulent melons of flesh"—as Peter The Poet had already written of them, too youthful yet to know such a metaphor was already an erotic cliche—apparent in the perfectly puckered roseate eye peeping out shyly through the silkenly furry cleft—The Poet, had he been there at that instant, would have instantly understood why the ancient Chinese, who knew a thing or two, referred to that part of the male anatomy as The Gate of Heaven.

As soon as he'd arrived in New York from Lima, Ohio, in the early 1970s, to make his fortune on Wall Street, Tom The Trickster had, having discovered in the second great vision of his young life the baths, bars, and backrooms of Manhattan, generously flung open that gate in those distant golden days of blissful ignorance and pleasure, inviting in all, the comely and uncomely, the young and the old (he'd been nothing if not democratic), in the incredible, word-defying ecstasy of playing the age-old game of Key-in-the-Back Door-Lock; unknowingly inviting in as well those microscopically invisible invaders that eventually made him HIV positive; made him, as mentioned, today, by choice, the moment he got the results of his AIDS diagnosis, as celibate as The Cardinal. Now he got what pleasure he once found in those ecstasies of the flesh in the pleasures of the unexpected—He had, in short, become The Jester, The Joker, The Monkey, The Trickster, a kid brother to all those rude, witty and revered figures of all primary peoples, of all our ancestors, who mainly now, he felt, sadly, were no more than pallid remnants weakly reflected in the plethora of stand-up comics on cable TV and in the comedy clubs, most of whom, Tom thought, "comforted the comfortable and afflicted the afflicted."

He saw his role as The Trickster with a somewhat different bent: to afflict the comfortable and comfort the afflicted.

He and Monsignor Malinowski would certainly have seen eye to eye.

Athletic in all his movements, he scrambled up now with the grace of a dancer and basketball player combined and stretched—the light now playing off the rippling lean muscles in his chest and thighs and down his back—and let his eyes wander up and down the length of his creation. Yes, it was all done now, letter-perfect. He would that very morning at The Demo to STOP THE CHURCH, as the posters read, unfurl his latest surprise from a most unlikely spot at The Cathedral, from the very heights of "that mausoleum of persecution/and repression," as The Poet called it in yet another one of those countless poems he was in the habit of sliding under Tom The Trickster's door.

Tom clicked off the lamp. In the dark, at the very instant that Peter The Poet, four floors above, was smiling down the barrel of the gun, Tom's impishly handsome face lit up in a wicked satyr-like grin.

He had danced the dance and had no regrets.

Also at that very moment, up in the rear top floor apartment behind The Poet's, its windows overlooking an empty lot that resembled a bombed-out site, but where sumac and Trees of Heaven and all manner of sturdy city weeds still pushed up among the mountains of trash and rubble from arsonist-burned and City-torn down tenements, "The Shamaness" (as Peter called her, tongue in cheek), a.k.a. Asmaralda, having just come back from leaving her daily steaming jar of special brew outside Tom The Trickster's door, now sat with her thin legs crossed on a soiled pillow in the middle of her completely bare back room, before a bowl of burning herbs. She was wearing a cheap black Edith Piaf-like dress; around her waist was a piece of old frayed rope, as frayed as her hair, serving as a belt, to which was attached a ring with many keys of assorted sizes riding on her skinny hip. Her kinky, frazzled gray hair was spread out in tall spikey points about her head and as she leaned toward the bowl, in its faint glow, the black-black skin of her tight, skeletal face shone like dark gleaming leather.

The only other objects in the room, besides the pillow on which she sat, were a collection of assorted jars and bottles and a small sterno stove in the corner on which constantly bubbled a pot of water in which she mixed her brews and tinctures.

She withdrew from a burlap bag at her side a long sewing needle with which she pricked the index finger-tip of her left hand and shaking the finger over the smoke, muttered, "*Oma, Oma,*" over and over, the drops of blood smoking in the sizzling bowl.

Growing silent, she drew her knees up and resting her sharp chin on her bony kneecaps, her black-black eyes darting like a bird's, she listened, and as she did, a smile opened her mouth, revealing among the strong white teeth, a gold front tooth with a diamond chip in its center, which sparkled in the wan coals of the burning herbs.

In that smile it was as if she knew everything.

Without leaving her pillow, she already knew, in her Mind's Eye, unlike The Poet, unlike The Trickster, busy with their own schemes, all that had gone on in The Chancellory that morning with The Cardinal, since, after the first announcement of The Demo, she checked in on him daily. She had, in the daily ritual of her out-of-body trance, already been several places around the city in the pre-dawn hours, having made her usual early visit to the children with AIDS ward at Lincoln Hospital in the South Bronx and at Harlem Hospital up on West 125th.

She leaned close to the fiery bowl of smouldering yellow dock, wild geranium root, witch hazel bark, mandrake root, and catnip, and closing her enormous frog-like eyes and breathing in deeply, murmured, "*Oma, Oma*," again and again. As she chanted, blue lights played along the peeling paint of the tin-embossed ceiling, and her spirit was transported now up through the very roof of the leaky old tenement and out once more over the city, where gulls, their underwings catching the first fire of early morning sun, were winging their way down the East River a block away toward the Brooklyn Bridge.

The spirit of Asmaralda was now in the wings of one of those birds, for she had learned long ago how to soar while sitting down.

No one knew where she came from; some said the West Indies, others said from Guyana. Still oth-

45

ers, like Tom The Trickster, playing the wag, winked, "Another planet"—"In a far, *far* outer galaxy," added The Poet, and they'd both got to giggling over that.

She never told, because she never divulged much if anything about herself. She was eerily quiet, kept to herself and when in the presence of others, which was rare—Tom The Trickster quipped, "Even when she's right before your very eyes she's not there"—always wearing her ring of unmatched keys, always clutching that grimy burlap bag of hers, she was unfailingly courteous.

She had simply appeared on the doorstep of the building late one night in April soon after they'd all moved in, in her cheap black dress and pointed hair, carrying that burlap sack "bulging with Goddess-knows what," as Deirdre The Rad Dyke, who lived on the third floor, put it. She had, as Tom and Peter and Deirdre, who were just returning from a combined ACT UP and WHAM! meeting over on 13th Street, stared in amazement, whispered her name then darted around to the side of the building, knowing somehow precisely where the secret entrance was, climbed the sagging stairs in the pitch dark to the top floor— that she appeared to know exactly where she was going and that she did it in total darkness, also amazed the trio as they followed her in with their tiny clip-on flashlights (also gifts from Tom) lighting their own way. She ensconced herself without a word in the last remaining, habitable apartment in the building: the one under the roof back of The Poet's—"So I be nearer the stars," as, in one of her rare moments of speech, she later told him, which he, being a poet, instantly understood.

She'd been there ever since.

Actually, for all her powers, Asmaralda had a rather humble start in life: born on a South Bronx sidewalk in the middle of the night to a heroin-addicted mother barely more than a child herself, who lived on the streets and who left her newborn baby there in her caul (a powerful foreboding of magical powers and luck), along with the afterbirth and the bloody umbilical cord, which she had bitten off before she hurried away, with the look in her dark eyes of a frightened animal who does not comprehend what has just happened to it.

The infant was found by a passing patrol car and rushed to the pediatric ward of Lincoln Hospital, where one of the Haitian nurses named her "Edith," for singer Edith Piaf, The Sparrow, also born in a street, in a Parisian slum.

It took the baby "Edith," twitching and bawling, quite some time to withdraw from her mother's addiction.

Then, from foster home to foster home, abused physically, sexually, used as a servant, used as a slave, even, until, at fourteen, "Edith," like her mother, hit the streets. But, unlike her mother, she kept, as if from those ingrained memories of infancy, away from drugs, from booze. She always seemed to make her way, panhandling or, grinning appealingly, holding doors open and carrying heavy grocery bags for people at neighborhood supermarkets, and even washing windshields with a rag and a squeegee for quarters as the heavy morning commuter traffic rolled off the George Washington Bridge up in the streets of Washington Heights.

No one came looking for her. She'd been on her own ever since.

It wasn't long after she'd been on her own that she had her first out-of-body experience as she was walking along Broadway one morning heading for McDonald's after her rush-hour squeegeeing, the pockets of her black dress bulging with quarters, along with her squeegee and her Windex bottle filled with water and ammonia, and her bit of rag. The power of it flattened her to the pavement. This enormous big-titted, broad-hipped black woman with a mouth full of gold teeth that sparkled with diamond chips when she smiled, a smile that was so dazzling it outshone the sun itself, reached for "Edith" and lifted her into her arms.

She said her name was Big Sister. She said if ever she wanted to reach her to call "Oma."

Minutes later, the paramedics picked "Edith" up out of the gutter into which she had rolled and jolted in her trance, and where her pockets had been picked clean of all her quarters by opportunistic passersby before the ambulance arrived, and rushed her to the emergency room at Columbia-Presbyterian. The doctors there said she was epileptic. She knew better. Intuitively, without words, without anyone telling her, she knew what it was.

Since she didn't have any money or medical insurance, they of course told her to go, giving her some medicine (phenobarbitol), which as soon as she was out of the ER, she dropped down the nearest sewer. Still light-headed but knowing that her pockets were empty, she headed north on Broadway back toward the George Washington Bridge, hoping to squeegee a few more windshields to get something to eat. As her head grew clearer, she was baffled to find herself clutching a grimy, bulging burlap sack in her left hand. She stepped into a doorway and when she peeked into the bag it appeared at first to be filled with nothing but assorted shades of dark and possibly used tea leaves, but the longer she stared, the more the "leaves" began to glow with a luminescent darkness.

She snapped shut the neck of the bag. Somehow, without knowing, she knew what they were. Somehow she knew what it was she had to do with those "tea leaves."

Passing the McDonald's at West 170th, where she always stopped each morning for an Egg McMuffin and a cup of black coffee after squeegeeing windshields, she caught a look at herself in the plateglass windows and saw that her hair was now standing out in star-points about her head, as if she'd stuck her finger in an electric socket. When she opened her mouth in amazement, she saw that one of her front teeth was now capped in gold and sported a diamond chip, just like Big Sister's, in her vision.

Tied around her waist on a frayed rope was the ring of keys.

Ever after that, all she knew was to hold onto the bag and that the keys tinkling on her hip opened everything. And it was soon after this that Big Sister appeared again to her, this time in a dream and told her to rename herself "Asmaralda." Never having liked the name given her at Lincoln Hospital, she gladly changed it.

Asmaralda—she liked the sound of it—all those "a's"—like the start of the alphabet, like the start of something.

After that, whenever she felt the power of Big Sister coming over her, she headed for some out of the way place, some cellar entry or back alleyway or a deserted building. At first, she never knew where Big Sister would take her, back to the South Bronx or to Harlem or down to Alphabet

City, but more and more, as she clutched the bag and held onto the keys, she knew.

It was just that Big Sister's visitations were so unexpected, so unpredictable sometimes, she realized she did need a place to be off the streets, a place to be safe and private, a home, really, to receive her, when the power in the guise of the enormous black woman chose to speak to her. It was in one of her trances that she had had a vision of the abandoned tenement on Avenue D, clearly seeing Tom The Trickster and Peter The Poet and Deirdre The Rad Dyke, and precisely where each one of them lived in that ramshackle building, and who they were and what they were doing. Most importantly, she saw every brick, board and window of the empty rear apartment behind The Poet's, under the roof and therefore "nearer the stars."

It was that very same night she had appeared on their doorstep. Even though she had had to wait several hours, she had been patient, standing in the shadow of the entry (she already had seen, in her vision, the camouflaged secret entrance at the side of the building). She knew that was where she belonged, where she had to be.

Where Big Sister sent her, she went.

Meanwhile, uptown in the gloomy but lavishly appointed Chancellory dining room, with its enormous crucifix leaning from the wainscoting directly over his head, The Cardinal, after rapidly crossing himself with an equally rapid prayer of thanksgiving (including giving thanks for his still-hearty appetite, glory be to God), with the sharp, highly polished tines of his fork (lovingly brought to a mirror shine, as with the hundreds of other pieces of the heavy, ornate Chancellory silverware, the first Saturday, without fail, of each and every month by Mrs. Rafferty herself) stabbed into the yolk of one of his over-easy eggs, preparing to begin what might well be his last breakfast on earth.

Deirdre, The Rad Dyke, loved her fat. She loved her big tits with their enormous purple nipples that had given so much pleasure to so many women, and lately, especially, to her beloved Kitty, her new-found love, whom she'd met at a benefit for WHAM!

Like Tom The Trickster on the first floor, she liked to work around her apartment in the nude, and as she sat on her rice prayer mat before a lighted pink candle in her rooms two floors above his, she meditated on The Goddess, gazing down on her ample flesh with gratitude, since she pictured The Goddess as a huge-huge woman, very much like herself.

She considered meditation and activism *her* work, *paying* work being hard for her to come by and, because of prospective employers' prejudice against her size, she had been grateful when Tom and Peter had befriended her at the ACT UP meetings, where she was a member of the Women's Committee, as well as WHAM!, and Tom, on learning she had no place to live (Kitty's place over on Prince Street was a shoebox, and Deirdre's monthly Welfare checks were also small, so she could never afford a place of her own, not even in Alphabet City), invited her to share the abandoned tenement on Avenue D.

"I am truly here in this solid flesh," she breathed, "thank Goddess," and breathed in the odors of herself, as she did each morning during her meditations—the good healthy womanly smell of her unshaved armpits, the milkily pungent odor of her breasts, emanating from hard "bite-sized" nipples, as Kitty kittenishly referred to them, to, since she was in estrus at that moment, the multitudinous subtle scents—at least 150 distinct ones, according to one research report she'd read—wafting up from her "rubyfruit jungle," her "quim," her "cunnie," all sweet descriptive words breathed sweetly, passionately, by her Kitty between kisses "down there," from which now the subtle aroma of wild flowers teased her nostrils, wild flower scents rising from a heady and delicate swampish hint of wetlands by the sea.

"*Down there,*" Deirdre sighed, unknowingly echoing The Cardinal, but in a thoroughly different context, naturally. She closed her eyes in remembrance. "Thank you, Goddess, for *down there.*"

She could sort out and identify intimately, just before that time of the month—the menses, the Moons of The Goddess, as she preferred to think of them—every blessed one of those 150 tantalizingly delicious aromas in the "honeypot"—*her* name for "down there"—of her beloved Kitty.

From below, the Latino and rap music drifted into her windows from the tape decks in the cars waiting to be repaired, or to have FLAT FIX, so much white noise that drifted in and out of her meditations. Earlier, from above, she'd heard Peter The Poet singing some incomprehensible aria out his window, as he often did, in retaliation, but because the insistent macho beat and offensive rap lyrics of the music had nothing to do with her own "lesbiana rhythms," as she liked to call them, she didn't let them bother her. She figured that if she let everything males do get to her, from their man-made made-for-men-only God—

Deirdre truly understood Mary Daly's dictum: "If God is male then male is God"—to their silly adolescent spank-the-monkey music, she'd end up as crazy as Anne Sexton and Sylvia Plath, and just as suicidal.

Those days when women were driven mad and to their deaths from men's madness were over, as far as she was concerned.

Her speculations on men had started innocently in her early teen years back in North Carolina: "Why are there no father-in-law jokes?" she asked herself. "Why are some women called 'man-haters' but you never hear, despite their being everywhere, any man called 'woman-hater'?"

Having begun to perceive then that, for women, the home front has always been the war front, that males, perennially adolescent, are oblivious to the consequences of their inventions, not to mention of their acts—life, to them, she saw, is an endless boy's game, with often lethal results—in her gradually evolved radical vision of a womanly world women, controlling the marketplace, would see to it that people had enough to eat, decent houses to live in, meaningful work, and the leisure for lively discourse and to make art, make poems in celebration, and otherwise invent, particularly the useful and beautiful. As for the majority of males, women, for thousands of years, had been trying to humanize them, and now she saw the hopelessness of it and was ready to admit defeat; so, in her women's world, she would have males do what males do best: she would, except for the wittiest faggots, including those, like Peter The Poet, who really knew how to dance, give them sticks and balls and paint and send them out into the green fields to play and paint their faces. In her female utopian paradise, occasionally males and females would come together for celebration festivals, a few selected males, those few who genuinely loved and respected women, would be let back in among the women who chose to mate (all the while, female biologists would, of course, be working day and night to relearn the secret of parthenogenesis), males selected for courage *for* life, and for their courage and imagination to embrace their womanly selves, males who were at one with The Goddess. Immediately after such unions, the males would be sent back to the green fields, where they would be continually watched over by fierce Amazons who would break up any power bondings, nip in the bud any secret schemes, any hints of the old traditional male paranoia and ninnyness, rooted in fear of each other—and of course of women. Then there would be once more on earth, "as it was in The Beginning," she devoutly believed, before the males caught on, only sons and brothers; and no more fathers with their obsession for ownership of everything, including children, and most certainly including women, not to mention Mother Earth herself.

The watchword of Deirdre's womanly world would be: EVOLVE INTELLIGENCE—an extremely scarce commodity, she concluded, in any patriarchy.

Such was her radical womanly vision for the future, which, everytime she meditated on it, as now, sent her gargantuan breasts shivering with delighted expectation.

In Deirdre's vision of a womanly society, the phallic "I" to determine the female would be changed to the vaginal "O," as in "O am a woman," "O am her story," and "O am here to stay," not far off Big Sister's "Oma," which Deirdre often heard Asmaralda in the apartment above chanting through the ceiling, figuring, mistakenly, it had something to do with *Santeria* or the occult. (Asmaralda simply smiled shyly and enigmatically whenever Deirdre questioned her about it.)

Unlike Asmaralda, who had no problems with nomenclature—Big Sister was Big Sister, *period*—Deirdre called the power she prayed to "Goddess." But she knew it was The Unknowable, The Unnamable. The Cardinal would've had a snit, but Deirdre also knew that man-made religions, while paying lip-service to The Mystery, usually with supernatural fireworks in technicolor à la The Wizard of Oz, still tried to make It knowable: To personify It in man's own image the better to rule the roost (Dr. Daly again). She wanted none of that; she called It "The Goddess" because it sounded better than just "It," and because she knew, to the depths of her Goddess-given fat, that It was, and is, first mover in the world, in the universe, as it was in the beginning and always was and always will be, not amen but ah women. Period.

Speaking of which, she thanked Goddess her own period wouldn't be for a few more days yet, anticipating her usual Sunday after-breakfast roll-around with her darling Kitty.

So, following the directions of her Goddess and becoming a mover rather than a victim, she preferred taking meaningful action in and for her life, and the lives of other women (as well as WHAM!, both she and Kitty also belonged to Women's Health Education Network, or WHEN) and, like just about everyone in the house that day, Deirdre The Rad Dyke had her own secret stratagem for The Demo at The Cathedral that morning: She planned to sock The Cardinal in the jaw.

Just thinking about it made her breathe more quickly, her nipples lifting to hard points.

"It'll be the sock heard round the world!" she gloated.

It would, she fervently believed, signal the end of all The Cardinal stood for, would signal the beginning of a new courage for all women. Or at least be a first tiny step. (Great oaks from tiny acorns, etc.) And if she had to spend time in jail, well, so what? It would be well worth it; and, besides, not that she was complaining but, after living in a hovel like the tenement on Avenue D, the slammer might seem like a deluxe resort—and, think of it, a resort filled with nothing but sweet honeypots!

She was breathing lightly, rapidly now, her armpits damp with hairy sweat, her cunnie suddenly, sweetly moist with exhilaration at not only the women-only prison fantasy but the daring of her plan for The Demo.

In preparation for which she had been taking free boxing lessons at The Women's Martial Arts Center in Brooklyn, spending hours punching the punching bag there, polishing her left hook. She'd gotten especially good with her haymaker and roundhouse right.

So, Deirdre The Rad Dyke and Peter The Poet, who was at that very moment fondling the barrel of the semi-automatic in the apartment directly above hers, shared, in their separate ways, something in common, including a rather innocent idealism, not to mention a decided taste for martyrdom.

She pressed her palms together, pressed them to her brow, then shut her eyes and leaned her massive body toward the single pink candle flame.

"Great Goddess," she prayed, "be with me."

Also at that very moment, in the top floor rear, still sitting on her pillow while she flew down the East River in the wings of a gull, to greet the sun, as she did each dawn, Asmaralda's head shot up, her eyes darting everywhere, as they did whenever one of the great ancient and ever-returning deities was evoked, whenever she, like an acutely sensitive radio receiver, plucked from the air waves an earnest prayer from the heart to that rainbow band of spirits, a prayer she often heard broadcast lately from the apartment directly below and that she now tuned in on once more as it radiated up through the sagging floorboards.

"*Oma,*" Asmaralda called and forked her fingers downward, like forked branches divining water.

Big Sister was in her.

Deirdre opened her eyes. She felt suddenly bolder, surer, knew to the depths of her great belly her prayer had been answered.

She checked her Timex watch. Because she lived not in man-made time but in the moon- and sun- and tidal times of The Goddess, in the rhythms of her own body in rhythm with the earth, she was late for everything, including ACT UP meetings. So the watch had been a gift from Tom The Trickster, who may have left the men's club of The Stock Exchange but still kept time to its clocks. So, being practical, whenever she had to be somewhere in man-made time, she wore the watch; when she didn't have to be anywhere, she took it off. And, just so she *could* wear it, her thoughtful Kitty had bought for her at a specialty shop uptown, "For The Big Woman," an extra long watch band to go around her sizable wrist.

She saw it was time to be getting ready for The

Demo. On her way, of course, she would first stop off at Kitty's where they'd have breakfast together . . . *and,* before the pair headed up to The Cathedral, who knew what else? she thought, with a flush of excitement.

As for her plan to sock The Cardinal, who, uptown in The Chancellory dining room, was at that very moment savoring a morsel of Mrs. Rafferty's done-to-perfection steak and kidneys, she hadn't breathed a word about it to Kitty; she knew it would only worry her.

She pulled herself up from the prayer mat and went off to the dark cubbyhole of a kitchen to the sink, walking with that lightness and grace that many large people have, and began, since she was already naked, giving herself a sponge bath from the bucket of water sitting in the sink, a bucket which, as mentioned earlier, was always filled for her and left outside the door by the thoughtful Peter up on the top floor every time he went down to the corner hydrant to fill up his own pail.

Not a bad lad, as lads go, thought Deirdre, who had continued to let him do it even though she was quite capable of hauling her own water—*and* Asmaralda's, if it came to that.

Since she was on an upper floor, she had windows, two in front overlooking Avenue D and two in the back bedroom (unlike The Poet she had washed her windows, getting herself out on the sills in a very tight squeeze to Windex the outside panes). Clean windows let in, as she put it, "the light of The Goddess in the sun."

Her apartment was not as sparsely furnished as The Poet's, or The Trickster's for that matter, having two unmatched oversized, over-upholstered easy chairs she had found at different times on the street and had carried home on her back (she was amazingly strong, not "Heinz 57"

58

for nothing, she liked to brag), and a queen-sized mattress—one she had spotted instantly that she and Kitty could really roll around on—discarded in the gutter over on 3rd Avenue. Checking it first for visible vermin, bedbugs, lice, fleas, etc., she'd also toted it home on her back and hauled it up the three flights of stairs to her apartment, where she'd disinfected it with Lysol, then scrubbed it to a faretheewell with lavender-scented carpet shampoo, making it clean and sweet-smelling, before she invited Kitty over to "christen" it.

They'd certainly done a lot of rolling around on it ever since.

A three-legged kitchen table with a heavily chipped porcelain top (the fourth "leg" was a pile of paperback lesbian mysteries Kitty'd brought over), a few unmatched kitchen chairs Deirdre had found here and there, or "the boys," as she called them, had found in the basement or in the streets and given to her—and her pride and joy: an enormous metal vegetable bin with metal doors to keep her food in (and keep the mice and rats out) that she'd found in the alley outside the greasy spoon on Avenue A, and which she'd carried home, disinfected and scrubbed inside and out and which now was her larder, holding what little food she could afford from her monthly Welfare check, which, since where she now lived was not officially an address, she had mailed to her care of Kitty's apartment.

After her sponge bath, she brushed her long wavy hair, hair which came well below her buttocks (small Kitty could just about cover herself in it), hair as black and shiny as a raven's wing, which Deirdre was convinced came from her Cherokee grandmother. Deirdre was from Hickory, North Carolina, and it was her mother who always said the family was "Heinz 57," with Deirdre being "the mos' Heinz 57 of us all, since you never know which branch of the family tree she's gonna' pop out of at you"—the Scots-Irish, the Cherokee, the Cuban ("Yezz," said her mother "there'd bin one 'a thim fellas sniffin' round back thin"), or "the smidge of color," which the mother referred to as "high yella," in a great-great-grandmother from Buncombe County.

Deirdre never bothered with underwear, and *never* a bra—underwear and bras in her size were too difficult to come by and even had she come by them, she couldn't afford them on the pittance Welfare paid her; mainly she believed the body should be allowed to *breathe,* as The Goddess intended, and that her sizable breasts be unfettered as well. Once she dried herself after her sponge bath, she pulled from the closet one of the several muu-muus she'd made herself, deciding on the bright orange one for this special day, and throwing it over her head, shimmied into it.

Stepping into a pair of well-worn, men-sized sneakers that she'd been practicing her boxing lessons in (she wanted good footing when she squared off before The Cardinal later that morning), completed her dressing. And since she was neither vain—nor fretted about what people thought of her size (most males are terrified of big women, she'd decided, which is why they want them all skinny as adolescent boys)—nor wore makeup (except when Kitty, when she was in one of her many kittenish moods, asked her to paint her lips a bright-bright red, then Kitty, more into femme because of her clerk's job, supplied her compact)—there was not a mirror, not even a chip of a one, to be found anywhere in her apartment.

But first, before leaving, she had to pee.

As for taking care of her own "biological functions," to pee, she straddled a bucket which she then emptied out the back window into the empty lot, or squatted, as she did now, out that self-same window (there was no one to see in the boarded up tenements across the empty lot). She noted, with satisfaction, the weedy growth, and especially the Tree of Heaven growing under the window, were doing particularly well.

As for the other, since she saw Kitty every day, she took care of that matter more conveniently over at her place.

Shutting the window, she patted herself dry with a natural honeycomb sponge, a gift from Kitty from Mother Nature's Own Health Food on West 23rd, shook her hips til her muu-muu shivered down below her knees, then slung her shoulder bag over her broad shoulder and before going out the door, took a deep breath, put her palms together again and placed them at her brow, murmuring once more for luck, "Great Goddess, be with me," then, after blowing out the candle, she feinted with her right and jabbed the air with her left, in one last practice punch.

Little did she know she'd get one more practice session in before she arrived at Kitty's.

Tom The Trickster had been the first to leave, wanting to get to The Cathedral as early as possible, while the streets around it were still relatively empty.

He had planned everything down to the last detail, as he had with all his previous climbs. His first had been an ascent, like a human fly, up the face of The Federal Court House Building in Foley Square, where, once he'd reached the fifteenth floor, he'd unfurled a banner reading: JUSTICE

FOR PERSONS WITH AIDS!; his most recent had been a climb up the cables of Brooklyn Bridge, where he'd dropped a banner from mid-span reading: BRIDGE THE GAP IN AIDS SPENDING!; then, as the TV cameras rolled from the helicopters above and on the crosswalks of the bridge below—he had learned how to manipulate The Media, who he'd alerted beforehand with each escapade, from keeping an eye on those two old pros, The Cardinal and The Mayor—he took a swan dive into the East River (surviving, unbeknownst to him, with the help of Asmaralda who appeared suddenly, and appropriately, as an enormous swan and floated him down). He spent only the night in jail for that one, til ACT UP bailed him out the next morning, while the Foley Square incident had cost him a day and a half in the pokey.

But in most of his other capers, because of careful planning, luck, and his incredible speed, he'd managed clean getaways.

He had already spent days, for instance, dressed inconspicuously in one of his old conservative business suits from his Wall Street days, which he'd saved for just such occasions, beginning with the earlier action at The Stock Exchange, poking about The Cathedral like any devout tourist, Polaroid camera ("compliments" of the Barbizon Photo Supply Shop on Lexington Avenue) slung around his neck, studying the edifice, its fancifully ornate stonework reminding him of sugar-spun icing on a wedding cake—"a *rotten* wedding cake," as The Poet had sneered in one of his under-the-door poems—observing it from all angles, especially the tall steeples at the main entrance, soaring several hundred feet into the air above 5th Avenue. He even went inside The Cathedral, to take a close look at the architecture of the gloomy vaulted ceiling, although he did not like the insides of churches, which he always thought of, as did The Poet, as mausoleums of the spirit.

Snapping away briskly, he'd also taken Polaroids of the roof and particularly the north steeple, then gone around to the rear of The Chancellory, which was attached to The Cathedral, back on Madison Avenue—where, unbeknownst to The Trickster, of course, inside at that very moment The Cardinal had been dressing and oiling up his pompadour for an appearance on The Phil Donahue Show that very afternoon, hoping to bring back into the fold that lovable but strayed Liberal apostate once and for all, with his dangerous utterances on Pro-Choice and The Disordered, to name only two of the main heresies that stuck in The Cardinal's craw.

Tom had taken notes as well and these, along with the photos, he had studied carefully under his wrought-iron lamp back at Avenue D, minutely plotting his ascent.

With his tightly muscled, wiry body, his grace and sure sense of balance, Tom The Trickster was a natural-born athlete, but not as a climber—in flat Ohio, there'd been no opportunity to learn that particular skill. So, before every one of his planned climbs, he worked out at The Face It, the latest yuppie diversion up on Madison Avenue, several blocks from the steeples of The Cathedral itself, in fact. It was an indoor rock-climbing establishment with an artificially constructed, sheer fifty-foot cliff face made of pre-cast and pre-stressed concrete which included gouged-out hand- and foot-holds that simulated as closely as possible, including their exact grainy, rough surfaces, those randomly come on on an actual rock face out in the natural world.

Knowing the owner, a blonde muscleman named Bob, hung like a satyr, with whom Tom had tricked any number of times in The Golden Days, he got his indoor climbing lessons for free, after hours—"For old buddies' sake," said Bob, after Tom had told him of his HIV status and self-avowed celibacy. Although Bob didn't mention it, he also did it for the pleasure of watching and working with Tom who, as always, whenever he could, except for the heavy backpack around his shoulders which he wore as he had before his previous ascents, for the practice (he mentioned not a word of what he was practicing for to Bob), worked, as he did at home, in the altogether, his bare skin gleaming with light perspiration.

Several nights a week, then, strapped in a safety harness, Tom had clamored agilely up the sheer face of the several-stories high artificial rock, grappling with the precarious holds with rosin-whitened fingers and Nike-sneakered toes.

Bob said he was the "fastest learning climber" he'd ever had.

Now, on the morning of The Demo, he began getting ready for his departure, first carefully folding up, starting at the unweighted end lying out on the kitchen floor, the seventy-five foot long red winged phallus of a banner and stuffing it in the bottom of his capacious pack. He tossed in a length of very thin but very strong nylon rope (another "contribution" from Rivera's Hardware over on Avenue B), just in case. Then he put in a stout leather window washer's safety belt he'd managed to whisk out the carelessly left ajar side sliding door of a MAID FOR YOU WINDOW CLEANING van ("Your Glass Is Our Task") up on

West 13th Street. Next, he popped in a box of rosin "borrowed" from The Face It when Bob wasn't looking, then several gross of rainbow-tinted condoms from ACT UP's generous supply. And lastly, in went a plastic bag of mixed dried fruit ("No Sulphur or Artificial Preservatives or Coloring"), a "gift" from Mother Nature's Own Health Food store on West 23rd, for quick energy if suddenly needed during his ascent.

Slipping on a clean white T-shirt and pair of levis, he slapped on a roofer's cap and buckled a belt of roofer's tools around his waist (both items acquired through another carelessly left open rear door of an emergency roofing repair truck over on 1st Avenue one recent late afternoon). He figured if anyone got suspicious at The Cathedral, he could always pause in his climb to unsnap a few tools and pretend to be fixing an "emergency leak" in The Cathedral's roof.

As he glanced around to see if he'd forgotten anything, he took a swig of the brew Asmaralda had left outside his door that dawn, then screwing the top tight on the jar, tucked it in his pack, since he knew climbing is thirsty work.

Everything in readiness, he zipped up his backpack, slipped it on to his back through the shoulder harness, unsnapped from a belt loop the clip-on penlite that he always carried with him, as did all the other squatters, except of course for Asmaralda, whose burning eyes lit paths in darkness, so he could see in the moldering, black-as-night passages leading from his apartment to the secret entrance at the side of the building. Once outside, squinting in the early morning sun that was just lifting over the roofs of the Lillian Wald housing projects across the street, he began jogging lightly, easily, down Avenue D, past the loud

65

salsa music and the Latinos lounging on the fenders of their cars, heading for the subway station over on Astor Place.

From above, still flying seated on her pillow, Asmaralda, with her sixth, seventh, and eighth senses, knew, just as she knew of all the comings and goings of the other inhabitants of the building, knew, in fact, of any dangerous intruders, such as junkies looking to bust in and turn their dilapidated home into a shooting gallery or a crack house, or, worse, cops or City fire or building inspectors come snooping around, and, with her forked fingers, acted accordingly—her watchfulness, unbeknownst to her other squatter neighbors, was the reason they had no need for locks—now knew that Tom The Trickster was leaving, knew exactly where he was going, and why.

Meanwhile, back in that gothic edifice toward which Tom The Trickster was heading, The Cardinal was polishing off his hearty breakfast alone at the enormously long table in the splendid dining room of The Chancellory, while up in The Cardinal's spacious private bathroom, Brother Francis was cleaning up after His Grace, energetically polishing the tub, the sink, and "the throne," til they were "white as the lambs of God," as he liked to put it.

Why Brother Francis had been late with The Cardinal's early tea, indeed was often late with it of a morning, was that he had had, as he often did at that hour, an errand to perform. Before dawn, before anyone else was awake and after he'd shined The Cardinal's shoes and had drawn The

Cardinal's piping hot bath, and while down on Avenue D Peter The Poet paced the floor and Tom The Trickster's eyes were just fluttering open, Brother Francis had crept down from his cell-like room under the severely sloping eaves of the roof of The Chancellory—the attic was a honeycomb of such cells for the servants (except for Mrs. Rafferty who adamantly refused to live in, insisting upon residing in her own apartment down on Avenue A, as she had with the late Mr. Rafferty for some forty years).

What Brother Francis was doing at that pre-dawn hour was ducking out to the public phone on the corner behind The Chancellory on Madison Avenue.

The good Brother was fully aware of how repulsive he was in The Cardinal's eyes, and fully aware as well of all the machiavellian machinations going on within The Chancellory between The Cardinal and The Mayor. These twin resentments had festered long and deeply within him, til be became, as a result, as scabrous in his spirit as he was in his flesh. No matter how mightily he prayed each night on his knees with bowed head at the side of his narrow cot up under The Chancellory roof, prayed even more mightily than The Cardinal himself when he asked for more Christian forbearance toward Brother Francis's skin condition, still, the Brother's conscience, not to mention his roaring resentments, nagged at him daily.

Brother Francis had another secret as well: Eavesdropping, as was his habit, outside The Cardinal's bathroom door (he had learned many of The Cardinal's inmost thoughts overhearing his mutterings as he went about his toilette, and it was often one more reason for the lateness of The Cardinal's morning tea), he had often heard His

67

Excellency growling about the late cardinal known as "Fanny"—it seemed to amount to an unholy obsession with him, thought the Brother. Yet Brother Francis, even though he knew it was a sin, found himself always taking "Fanny's" side, even felt a twinge of envy, as he heard The Cardinal, time after time, recite, behind the closed bathroom door, the litany of "Fanny's" misdoings.

When such twinges stirred the Brother, he blushed redder than the psoriasis spots on his tonsured scalp and, dropping everything, would immediately rush up to his cell where he would sink to his knees by his cot and fervently pray for forgiveness.

What he also occasionally prayed for forgiveness for were those early morning phone calls, which were anonymous messages he left in a disguised voice (he did a pretty good imitation of The Cardinal) on the answering machines of Dignity and ACT UP, giving detailed information of what exactly was going on within the walls of the Chancellory between The Cardinal and His Honor, The Mayor.

Despite his "God's eyes," The Cardinal hadn't the foggiest that he had a veritable "devil's eye," as he would have termed it had he known, serving him his morning tea and drawing his morning bath and now putting the finishing touches on polishing, til it gleamed, the old oak seat of The Cardinal's own personal "throne."

Down in the Astor Place subway station, one wall on one side of the token booth was plastered with handbills proclaiming STOP THE CHURCH, with their profile of The Cardinal in his miter and the announcement of that morning's Demo at The Cathedral, while the wall on the other side of the booth was plastered with handbills, announcing a Kiss-in at 6th Avenue and 8th Street, that included a black and white photo of two U.S. sailors with their arms around each other, kissing, and underneath it the words: READ MY LIPS.

Tom The Trickster, scanning the now-familiar posters with satisfaction til he heard the distant roar of the approaching Number 6 Uptown train, waited til the train came to a stop in the station and the doors opened before he leapt the turnstile and raced across the platform into the nearest car. (He'd only been caught once, and by a transit cop who, as luck would have it, thanks to the intuitive intercession of Asmaralda envisioning it beforehand on her pillow, he'd once tricked with and who also, evidently still remembering those Golden Days, let him go with a wink and a warning.)

On the ride uptown, he pulled out the photos he'd taken of The Cathedral, on each of which he'd marked with a green magic marker (not for Saint Patrick but, for the luck of it, for the ancient faggot Green Man) the best possible route to the north steeple, studying them one last time.

While he was bent over his photos, a homeless beggar in foul-smelling rags weaved down the center of the car, on his scarred and unshaven face, brutalized, it appeared, from years of living on the hard Manhattan streets, an expression of permanent stupefaction. Clutching the overhead hand rail in his bony fingers, he swung back and forth in front of Tom, thrusting in his face a crumpled and finger-smudged paper coffee cup and rattling the few coins at its bottom to gain Tom's attention. But The Trickster, like all the other passengers the beggar had already approached who, wrinkling their noses in distaste, had suddenly become intensely absorbed in their Sunday editions of the *Daily News* or *New York Times,* or in reading the subway ads or in studying their fingernails, was so wrapped up in his photos of The Cathedral, the roofs of which he'd be climbing over minutes after he left the subway, he neither saw, nor smelled, the man.

Nor did he notice, in the seat directly across, a surprisingly attractive, rather well-built youth, masturbating solemnly, his unfocused eyes filled with a dull and distant expression.

Nor was he aware of a gang of youths, evidently returning home and still all fired up from dancing at one of the all-night downtown dance clubs, who burst in at one end of the car, boogying and laughing as they swept through, snatching the gold chains from every throat that boasted one, most of the previously apathetic passengers now jumping up and screaming in panic until the gang exited at the other end.

He did look up, however, with the sure instinct of a long-time IRT subway rider, when the train pulled into his stop at the 51st Street station. Slipping the photos back into his pack, he leapt through the opening doors and darted up the stairs into the near-empty, early Sunday morning streets of midtown Manhattan.

Up on the top floor, Peter The Poet was also preparing to leave for The Demo. Like Deirdre below, he had taken a hasty sponge bath from the bucket of water reserved for that purpose in the sink, but afterwards, unlike Deirdre, had slipped into clean underwear, a pair of lavender very brief briefs. He figured, after his certain arrest later that morning, even though it went against his belief that a dirty poet was a better poet, it would make a favorable impression on his jailers if he were reasonably clean and had on presentable underwear, just as his mother had always taught him and his brothers and sisters, that in case accidents or other emergencies occurred (such as in this case his impending arrest), even if you're lying dead on the highway, people will know from your personal hygiene and the cleanliness of your "unmentionables," as she called them, that you come from a "respectable family," which to her was synonymous with "Catholic family."

Old lessons die hard, he thought. Old lessons of the mothers and fathers, in particular.

He would have packed an extra pair of shorts, but his lavender briefs were his only pair of *good* underwear because they had been the most recently "acquired," from the pricey Fire Island Pines Boutique on Christopher Street. The rest of his "unmentionables," which were from his days at Pearl River High School and which he'd brought from home when he'd left, were so tattered and tattle-tale gray by now he knew he would be ashamed to be seen in them, even in jail.

In his middle-class squeamishness, he realized he had a ways to go before he became, à la Rimbaud, whose own mother was no slouch when it came to petit-bourgeois ways, a totally "Bad-Assed Faggot Poet."

As if to prove that fact, he suddenly felt so fluttery, as though a cloud of butterflies was hovering in his belly. He glanced at his Timex and saw the morning was getting on. Wanting to have a good place in the front ranks of the demonstrators, one that would give him a good vantage point to draw his bead on The Cardinal—the very thought turned his knees to jelly, and, as The Cardinal had gripped the sink earlier, Peter now grabbed onto his writing table for support—he knew he better get cracking, since it was a long hike up to The Cathedral.

Since he walked everywhere in the city, believing poets (again, à la Rimbaud) should be peripatetic so as not to miss a trick, even on their way to an assassination, and also because he simply never had the fare whenever he needed to go somewhere (he lacked the nerve and swift agility of Tom The Trickster to hurdle the turnstiles), he would walk from Alphabet City the nearly 60 blocks up to The Demo. The hike might also help him work off that bad case of jitters that was surging through him, plucking madly at every nerve in his body.

At times like this he wished he had Tom The Trickster's guts. He loved the airy flights of poesy but catch *him* fly-walking up the side of a skyscraper to drop a message to the world! Anything higher than the second step of a ladder gave him vertigo.

And here he was, barely hours away from squeezing the trigger on The Cardinal!

He shut his eyes and tried to imagine what Tom's courage was like. But he couldn't.

Knowing he'd feel less jumpy once he got going, he began quickly packing his knapsack.

Envisioning his arrest, and probable rape, in The Tombs—having read Herman Melville's "Bartleby the Scrivener," he was certain that that was where he would be imprisoned—he was prepared: Into his knapsack, which was stuck with every conceivable political button from ACT UP and gay and feminist groups, he packed a recently "found" giant-sized tube of KY lubricant and a gross of lavender-scented, pre-lubed condoms (lifted from The Pleasure Chest over on 7th Avenue). In spite of Tom The Trickster's trying to street-smarten him up, he was still so green he didn't realize that the first thing that would be confiscated by prison authorities in any New York City jail—in any jail or prison anywhere in the USA, for that matter—was these very rubber goods, since jailers would rather risk, as indeed would The Cardinal himself, in jail or out of jail, the spread of AIDS and other venereal diseases in prisons than to appear, by the dispensing of such prophylactics, to condone The Great and Abominable Sin of Sodomy, Buggery, Butt-Fucking, Takin' a Hike Up the Ole Hershey Trail, which (and this The Poet wasn't green about at all), as all good American sons are taught at their father's knee, is a penetrating fate worse than death (as it very well could be in these days of The Plague, so that The Poet's watchword was "No glove, no love").

But because he was, unlike Tom The Trickster, naive about jail-time, in went his "gloves," the condoms, and the KY.

"O sodomio," he hummed, as he busily continued packing his knapsack, "O sodomio," which for him, at that moment, was akin to whistling in the dark.

In went a sheaf of scrap paper and a couple of BIC pens; then, realizing how boring life in a cell would be (he hadn't watched every rerun of Truman Capote's *The Glass House* on TV for nothing), he also tucked in, reverently, as if it were a holy relic, his autographed bible of The Golden Days: his dog-earred, much-stained copy of *A Day and a Night at the Baths*.

Then, the final, the most important item to be packed. He went into the kitchen and stood a moment staring up into the gloom at the sagging cabinet doors over the sink. He took a deep breath and then, as he had earlier that morning, as he had so many times before and now for the final time, carefully slid the semi-automatic pistol off its top shelf. Never once taking his eyes off it, as if it might suddenly leap into life, he carried it in his open palm to the front room where, his fingers closing firmly over it, he shut his eyes and quickly tucked it ever so gingerly under his copy of the baths novel.

Then he zippered the bag shut and stood up and faced the blond light glowing wanly in the soot-dirty panes of the front windows. He glanced again nervously at his watch.

Time to go. He took one last look around the place. "Goodbye, old *atelier*," he whispered, then, slinging his knapsack over his shoulder, he headed out the door, thinking, Well, if nothing else, at least in jail I'll get a room, three squares a day, and plenty of time to write my poems—if I live.

Flicking on his penlite, he crept down the dark stairs and when he got to the first floor, tiptoed past Tom The Trickster's door, wanting of course to slip off to The Demo alone, unaware that Tom had already left and was at that very moment, in his roofer's cap and roofer's tool belt, rounding the corner onto Madison Avenue, behind The Chancellory, passing the pay phone that Brother Francis had used to make his secret call only hours before.

In the meantime, within the pearl-gray stone walls of that very edifice, having downed the last of his morning tea, The Cardinal was leaning back in his hand-carved high-backed chair at the dining room table and contentedly folding his hands across his belly, a slight belch escaping his lips; while upstairs in The Cardinal's private bath, Brother Francis, having finished his tidying up and making everything gleam to a faretheewell, was quietly opening the ancient medicine chest and, just as he did each and every morning, he unscrewed the lid from His Grace's Wildroot Cream Oil bottle and, squirting a dab in his palm, rubbed it briskly into the thinning strawberry-blonde hair atop his own tonsured pate.

Once he'd slipped out through the camouflaged entrance at the side of the building, The Poet, squinting in the now bright sunlight pouring over the rooftops of the Lillian Wald projects across the way, cut north up Avenue D at a brisk gait. He checked his Timex again and figured if he kept to this pace he should make the eight long blocks crosstown and the fifty or so short blocks uptown to The Cathedral in about an hour, stopping first of course at The Shrine on West 28th Street. In spite of all his agitation, he had decided weeks before he would most definitely stop at The Shrine on the way and pay his respects, perhaps his last respects, on this most momentous morning of his life.

Already at that hour and even though it was Sunday, Avenue D was lined, bumper to bumper, with even more cars and livery cabs than earlier, either waiting to get repairs by the regular on-the-spot mechanics or getting washed by their owners from pails of water gotten from the corner hydrant, thanks to Tom The Trickster and his handy firefighter's wrench.

None of the cars were brand-new; in fact, the perpetual lineup of autos resembled a used car lot; if a new and very expensive automobile—a BMW or Mercedez-Benz—tooled down these streets, you could bet it belonged to a drug dealer, and often a dealer still in his teens.

Just as when Tom The Trickster jogged by earlier, the Latino men were gathered in little knots,
or leaned against the fenders of their cars, smoking, already drinking cans of beer wrapped in
little brown bags (it was, after all, a Sunday, a day
of rest), laughing loudly, greeting each new-
comer with high hand slaps, at ease with each
other, yet talking Spanish in quick, shrill voices
(when Peter first moved to the neighborhood, he
thought they were arguing all the time; he didn't
know this was simply the tone for normal, everyday affectionate ribbing and talk); and listening,
always listening, with some third ear, Peter
thought, to the merengue and Latin love songs
blasting out of their tape decks, dreaming,
maybe, in the music, he liked to think, since he
was a poet, of tropical islands, of rain forests, of
long, sultry tropical nights heavy with the per-
fume of massive, ponderous blossoms under
equatorial moons, dreaming it here on the hard
mean streets of Alphabet City, dreaming the illu-
sion of being safe in their banding together on the
sidewalks (Deirdre's Amazons would've certainly
broken *that* up), in their constant, reassuring
touches.

How they loved to be together! How they loved
each other's company, loved to casually touch
each other's warm, brown skin—like touching
the earth of home, thought The Poet, in another
of his poetic flights—or playfully slap hands or
tenderly punch each other—How relaxedly phys-
ical they were with each other, The Poet, as always, observed with envy, even much more so
than many gay males were; certainly much more
than he had been with his own brothers (touch
didn't run in his family)—And yet . . . and yet . . .

"*Homosocials,*" Peter called them, loving to be

76

together more than they love being with women, loving to do everything together but fuck.

They only noticed The Poet when he hollered incomprehensibly out his window, *el pato, el loco maricōn gringo.* Here, on the street, in his chalky white skin and scrawny, underfed body, they paid no attention to him: He was Other, the Stranger, and therefore didn't count. He was invisible to them. Only *they* counted, the familiar sweet music of Spanish, the familiar, comforting sounds of their native tongue in their ears, and the touch of their warm brown skins, their close bonding in a deep and undivided brotherhood shutting out any who were not like them: exclusive in their maleness rather than the inclusive vision of males Peter The Poet, à la Walt Whitman, envisioned, the inclusive vision of all, or as Peter had recently penned and now quoted aloud:

"Women loving women and men loving men
and men loving women and women loving men
must be
as one again"

Now passing the overpopulated, in his eyes, Lillian Wald and Jacob Riis housing projects, he thought of an article he'd read in *OutWeek,* and agreed with, about the great breeder religions, such as the one he'd been reared in, their "spiritual" root being an obsession with numbers, and therefore subverting and perverting the natural impulse of males loving to be with males (the Latinos on his block again) and of females loving to be with females (as it would be in Deirdre's utopian paradise). Like the bonobo, the pygmy monkey of Africa, no longer locked in an "eternal

77

present," no longer locked in seasonal hormonal floods, human fucking, as the article had pointed out, is primarily for pleasure, not procreation.

On this point, Tom The Trickster, for once, had agreed with The Poet. (One can only imagine The Cardinal's blood pressure had he been privy to it.)

As Peter crossed East 3rd Street, he could hear, several blocks ahead on the other side of Avenue D, a "ghetto blaster"—it seemed all chrome it was so big and shiny—blasting out rap lyrics at top volume on the slender shoulder of a teenager as he bopped along in front of the Jacob Riis projects.

> *Keep your looks offa me*
> *You Village queer*
> *If you don't want an icepick*
> *Up your rear*

Although such lyrics, as heard earlier blaring up from the tape decks in the cars below his windows, were nothing new to The Poet, still, he winced as they assaulted his ears yet one more time, and, as if someone struck him a blow from behind, hunched up his shoulders.

His antennae up for new ways to say it, he listened to rap tapes whenever he could, had even written a few "white boy raps" himself—because he also knew it was not only important to hear other ways to say it but also to know how *not* to say it—in short, to know your enemies. It's why he watched "the 'phobes" on his little black and white TV—they seemed, like The Cardinal, to be on every channel these days, homophobia being "the last respectable bigotry," one more on-target reason, he was convinced, to blow The Cardinal away. It's why he listened to rap lyrics like the one he was hearing right that very moment riding on the slim shoulder of the youth across the avenue, a rap he recognized as "Who Ya Winkin' At?" by Macho Two; he knew all this because he occasionally also filched the odd fanzine from the newsstands along with his daily *New York Times.*

He thought of the semi-automatic in his knapsack, fully loaded. He could right then get in some target practice before aiming at The Cardinal, if nothing else shoot a bullet straight at the Loudmouth speaker and through the heart of that ear-mugging rap cassette, silencing it forever. Because hearing those lyrics flooding the air, a sudden blood-red fury drowned out all reason, all fear. He saw himself clutching his semi-automatic and mowing down row after row of any number of Presidents and Popes, any number of Cardinals, any number of those who had climbed to power and privilege by polluting the air, polluting ears, with like twisted words—

> *"Sticks and stones*
> *Can break my bones,"*

he sang out in the direction of the music.

"And so can words," he added.

Being American to his fingertips, and a poet, speaking of contradictions, he thoroughly understood the compatriot who walks into a crowded McDonald's fast food or onto a children's schoolyard at recess or into a packed shopping mall and puts away twenty or thirty with an Uzi newly purchased at Moe's Friendly Gun Emporium, All Credit Cards Cheerfully Accepted.

"Such a quiet boy . . . such a quiet girl . . . Such a *nice* lad, an Eagle Scout, always so willing to help . . . church-going . . . Such a sweetheart of a gal . . ."

He could do that. He knew he could. Violent,

murderous, innocent, he could be just as American.

If Deirdre's punch would be the sock heard round the world, his would be the shot.

Instead of reaching for his gun, however, he cupped his hands to his mouth and shouted at the youth toting the blaster, "GO READ A BOOK!" but of course the rap music was so loud the youth didn't hear a word of it.

Even so, Peter carried himself now as if he had suddenly received an infusion of steel in his backbone, as he hurried on up Avenue D, the rap lyrics fading in the distance.

At East 9th Street somebody had spray painted in bright red on a boarded up store front: GASS FAGS. "Obviously a louse who's also a lousy speller," thought The Poet, who, "faster than a speeding bullet," unsnapped his own handy spray-paint can of Krylon lavender (also "compliments" of Rivera's Hardware) that he always carried in one of the side pockets of his knapsack, and giving the can a couple of hearty shakes, aerosoled the words to read: KISS FAGS.

After that, he bounced along like he had springs in his heels, only to be confronted on the corner of East 11th with another spray-painted message, appearing to be by the same hand, on a red, white and blue mailbox: FUCK A DIKE MAKE A WOMMAN OF HERR. The Poet, whipping out his can once more, simply inserted, correcting the bad spelling as he sprayed: ALL WOMEN: FUCK A DYKE—MAKE A HAPPY WOMAN OF HER! and continued bouncing on his way.

As he turned off Avenue D, he could hear a brand-new hot-red sports model car thumping down 14th, its stereo loudness blasting from the numerous loudspeakers, custom-installed, no doubt, in the trunk and in the back, where, as The Poet saw as the auto cruised closer, the backseat had been removed to make room for the additional speakers—the cost of which, he had read in a hi-tech music mag he'd swiped once with his morning *Times,* can reach as high as $20,000; speakers and car, no doubt, compliments of drug hustling in the projects; speakers thumping with another rap lyric, the words clear to the ears of The Poet, even though all the car windows were rolled up tight for the maximum ear-shattering effect within:

> *Queers,*
> *Save the planet*
> *from genocide*
> *commit suicide*
> *commit suicide . . .*

These lyrics he recognized as being by the rap group DCJAX and, in protest and in a futile attempt to clear the air, he sang out loud—with no hyped electronic boosters—The Shirelles' lyric, "*Stop the music, stop the music! . . .*" But his own lone human voice was no match for the State of the Art, total electronic assault roaring from the sealed car, and as it tooled past The Poet in all its gleaming splendor, making a turn down Avenue D into Alphabet City, The Poet continued to stubbornly sing back; but the beardless adolescent behind the wheel, his head bobbing to the beat, a rapt, stoned expression on his face, looked oblivious to everything.

Along East 14th, hordes of Sunday morning customers were out early pawing for bargains through the bins of merchandise spilling out onto the wide sidewalk. As he hurried past, The Poet suddenly had a vision of all the passersby crowding by him as nothing but lips, great, fat succulent American lips, sucking up everything in sight: polyester clothes and plastic shoes, right in their boxes; clothes and shoes of every imaginable color and size; saw them gobbling up gigantic TV's and VCR's and video and audio cassettes and sacchrinely sentimental religious pictures and popish trinkets; saw them gobbling up enormous hamburgers, cheeseburgers, tacos, shish kebab, baby back ribs, T-bone steaks, plastic wrappings and all; saw all those crowding around him as lips, sucking and smacking, lips gobbling up everything.

He was glad, at Union Square, to swing north on Broadway, and as it veered further west into Chelsea, he began to notice that the posters plastered on the walls and the grafitti chalked and spray-painted on the sides of the buildings and on the pavements were quite different from those he mainly saw in Alphabet City. He spotted on an empty building a rather ubiquitous poster at that time, the same one Tom The Trickster had seen down in the subway station earlier that morning, of two sailors kissing, plus another nearby of two women doing the same, and beneath each: READ MY LIPS. Beneath the poster announcing the KISS-IN in the Village, someone had scrawled in chalk: SAME-SEX KISSING FOR A TRULY KINDER, GENTLER NATION, another play on an election slogan made up for, as Tom called him, The Corporate President.

A block or so ahead Peter noted an older man with long, straggly locks and a floppy wide-brimmed forest-green felt hat and enough slogan buttons, even more than The Poet had pinned on his own knapsack, down the back of his frayed levi jacket to open a button store. He was crouching at every corner to hastily spray-paint a stenciled sign on the sidewalk. When Peter got to the next corner he glanced down at the curb to see what it was: RELIGION IS THE ENEMY! Peter recognized it as one of the sayings from his archival reading of Boston's old *Fag Rag,* one that the editors and writers of that radical paper had once carried on a curb-to-curb banner (the following year the banner read simply: COCKSUCKERS), in one of the Pride marches of the 70's.

Those were the days, sighed The Poet, and the face of The Cardinal loomed before his eyes, a face synonymous to him with the words crudely stenciled on the sidewalk, and he hitched up his knapsack, feeling the heft of the semi-automatic within, as he hurried on his way.

The older spray painter in the floppy hat was obviously a hold-over from that time—The Poet wondered if he too, like so many others, had been a habitué of The Shrine, one of the "old priests" of Priapus and Prepuce, one of the old worshipers. In those Golden Days, recounted in the novel tucked away beneath the pistol riding in his knapsack, had he been around, The Poet himself would have been most definitely an acolyte, at the very least, of Priapus.

The older man also appeared to be heading, appropriately enough, for The Demo, as were any number of others on both sides of the street, who, with placards on posts and furled banners, were also making their way up Broadway in the direction of The Cathedral.

Among them were the Latino/Indian lads he saw all over Manhattan, several of them now pushing their *supermercado* shopping carts uptown, carts filled with bouquets of gladiolas almost as tall as themselves; heading for the crowds at The Demo, no doubt, and hoping for brisk sales. They all seemed to have the same beautiful copper-reddish skin that gleamed in the sun, noted Peter The Poet admiringly, as he always did whenever he saw one, suspecting they were probably all "illegals."

"*Pato,*" one whispered to him, noting Peter's glances as he rattled his cart past. "Ey, *pato!* Three buck a bunch."

All gringos were queers.

Peter turned his pockets inside out. 50¢ in nickels and dimes. He wouldn't need money in jail, he decided, and what would be more fitting for his visit to The Shrine, so he held up a finger and shot the flower vendor a querying glance. The lad grinned and slipped a single red gladiola blossom from one of the bouquets and handed it to The Poet, who forked over his money and, saluting the boy with a smile, clenched the flower in one hand and continued on up Broadway.

Peter now noted that one of the activists heading uptown on the opposite side of the street was holding aloft a huge poster which read in red block letters: KNOW YOUR SCUMBAGS, and beside it a publicity headshot of an unctuously smiling Cardinal in his clerical drag including tall miter headdress, beside which was a shot of a large pink, unrolled condom, its "tickler" tip matching the crown of The Cardinal's miter, and beneath the condom the words: THIS ONE PREVENTS AIDS.

Peter liked the wittily irreverent comparison on the poster, which very cleverly made its point, and agreed with calling The Cardinal a "scumbag," but, being a poet and, hence, filled with the sacredness of all things (except, it seemed, for the life of His Eminence, of course), he resented the denigration of what the condom caught: cum as scum—sperm to him being "a sacred essence," not to mention an acquired taste, "like oysters," he thought.

But, then, that is the way with poets.

Next, his eye was naturally caught (the artist undoubtedly relying on it) by another black and white photo, this time stuck to a lamp post, of a roaring hard-on, where every vein was glisteningly visible along the quite lengthy shaft, and alongside it the words:

> MEN:
> Use Condoms
> Or Beat It.

Peter recognized it as the work of the artists' collaborative Gran Fury, which was sticking its work all over Manhattan.

There were not only many traditional SILENCE = DEATH stickers and posters but also a new one: ACTION = LIFE; and on the next lamp post Peter came to was a poster that gave him pause, which read simply: WANTED FOR MURDER, with a black and white mugshot of The Cardinal underneath.

Suddenly he saw his own mugshot replacing The Cardinal's and envisioned his own WANTED poster tacked up not only in the Pearl River Post Office but in post offices all over the United States.

That is, in case he got away. He was certain, however, because he was convinced he lacked the speed and wit of Tom The Trickster, once he squeezed the trigger, he would not.

This thought caused the butterflies to start swarming in his belly again, and he quickened his pace to try to settle them down.

On the very next lamp post was another poster, this one with a glum, funereal photo of the bushy-haired Mayor, The Cardinal's dearest, most intimate friend, and beneath it the words: DEATH IN THE CLOSET. CLOSETS KILL.

And everywhere were stickers that read: SOMEONE WITH AIDS WAS HERE.

And equally everywhere, just as Tom The Trickster had seen earlier in the subway, The Poet saw STOP THE CHURCH posters, hundreds of which had been pasted up all over the Lower East Side and Chelsea and the East Village and the West Village in past weeks to announce that morning's Demo. Each showed yet another photo of The Cardinal wearing his miter headdress with tail-flap, and highlighting, in careful key lighting on beak and brow, like a Hollywood publicity shot, the profile of which, with its aquiline nose, The Poet had heard, His Eminence was inordinately vain.

Underneath, in smaller caps, the STOP THE CHURCH poster proclaimed:

FIGHT ITS OPPOSITION TO ABORTION.

FIGHT ITS MURDEROUS AIDS POLICY.

TAKE DIRECT ACTION.

TAKE CONTROL OF YOUR BODY.

ACT UP

WHAM!

As he re-read the words on the poster, The Poet reached back and patted the knapsack where the semi-automatic rested, and as he continued up Broadway, he tucked the gladiola blossom behind his ear and marched rimrod-stiff, as if he'd received another infusion of steel in his spine.

As part of his plan, as mentioned earlier, The Poet made a left on West 28th Street and making his way to the middle of the block, paused reverently before The Shrine. What he was standing before was in actuality only what remained of The Shrine, which was the arching portal of its entrance and the recast concrete molding of the upper two floors of the Romanesque facade, a facade that had been renovated after the May 25, 1977 fire within that had killed a number of men. The sign across the front now read EVERGREEN MART, an Asian-American owned mini mall for wholesalers, but to The Poet, it was a sacred site: the site for over a hundred years of the old Everard Baths.

It had been shut down long ago in the early days of The Plague by The Mayor, a Mayor whom some accused, as intimated by the earlier-seen poster, of being a terminal closet case, and who, under the politically expedient guise of appearing to be doing *something, anything,* about the spread of this then totally mysterious disease, to appease an alarmed not to mention homophobic citizenry—it was right from the start known as "The Gay Disease"—had, after first sending spies posing as "customers" into the Everard who then reported—some said in "vivid detail"—back to His Honor—the Everard Baths and all such places closed by order of the Public Health Department, thus ending the days and especially the nights of one of the oldest and most notoriously world-famous Pleasure Palaces in all of New York City.

What better thing to do, The Poet had decided, on his way to assassinate the one whom he considered to be one of the behind-the-scenes architects of that murderous neglect in present-day City affairs of the living and the dying, than to pause in this very spot to pay homage to a great and illustrious, even, to The Poet, "holy" gay past.

Peter, of course, had been too young to have visited the baths—in the early 1980's, the time of their closing, he was only twelve years old and

still tear-assing around the idyllic suburban
streets of Pearl River, New York, on his bike, tossing the *Rockland County Journal-News* up on
well-manicured front lawns, while out of the corner of his eye, secretly, hungrily, admiring the
bronzed shirtless lads who, their leanly muscled
shoulders gleaming with summer sweat, were
pushing gas-powered mowers over those very
same lawns.

He had only read about those Golden Days of
the baths in such books as the all-too-slender, to
his mind, *A Day and a Night at the Baths,* his personal copy as well-thumbed as a Fundamentalist's
Bible (he had had to Scotch tape the paper cover
back on any number of times), which he now
slipped out of his knapsack and, eyes closed, held
up in a worshipful and prayerful manner to what
remained of the ancient portal of the old Shrine.
That gateway was also the photo on the cover of
the book, where, in other, long-ago days, starting
in the late 19th century, tens and tens of thousands of men had entered its hushed and steamy
darkness—Yes, and in later decades many more
tens and tens of thousands passing under those
same portals on their way out, in the pre-dawn
hours, after having barefootedly prowled those
endless dark halls hour after hour, searching for
that holiest of connections, and leaving blissfully
exhausted, but filled with new heart for the day,
so many unknowingly carrying within them, "in
the sacred sap of pleasure/that filled them," as
The Poet had phrased it in one of his poems, paraphrasing the, then, equally innocent author of
the baths novel—Who at that time could have
prophesied the imminent Plague?—the tattered
copy of which The Poet was now holding up before him in tribute (in just the same way The Cardinal would, an hour hence, be lifting The Host

on the altar of The Cathedral—for the last time, if The Poet had his way), while The Poet plucked from his ear and held aloft in his other hand the bright red gladiola—Yes, so many of these innocents carrying within them, from any one of a dozen anonymous lovers in the dark, the microscopic seed, the invisible virus, that in time would mean their terrible and undreamed of death.

So The Poet came to this moment with a mixture of gratitude and grief, not forgetting the decades of joys experienced by the throngs of men of all colors and from all over these States, all over the globe in fact, but always being keenly aware, as now, of the tragedy that took place here (the tragic fire of 1977 paling in comparison), an invisible tragedy, perhaps carried from other places (it does not matter from where) that worked its way secretly, silently, in the dark of this venerable cathedral of pleasure into the darkness of the blood of so many of the innocent, in the very instant of light-bursting rapture.

Suddenly, with the help of Asmaralda who, still seated on her grimy pillow in her top-floor apartment back on Avenue D, was now flying in the tiny, hotly beating heart of a common street sparrow far above the site of the old Everard, and spotting The Poet, whom she'd been tracking on his hike uptown, now flew down and, while The Poet stood raptly on the sidewalk with eyes shut fast, praying, with the ragged paperback book and the flower lifted high above his head, for all the living and the dead who had ever entered the portals of that sacred place, landed on his shoulder and giving him a little peck on the left ear, sent him into a deep trance, giving him a vision, a gift, really, of the paradise of After-AIDS:

And there they all were at the long-gone but now, in the spell in The Poet's eyes, paradisiacal

Everard Baths, which was floating high above West 28th Street on a huge heavenly cloud of hellish steam-room steam, all the long-gone once again crowded and flitting in their spiritual bodies through the long-abandoned dorms, through the long-abandoned cubicles and steam and sauna rooms (the latter, in the bowels of the basement, the hell of the place), the long once-dark corridors all aglow now with a rosy light, all alive and populated again with naked males in ghostly white bath towels, prowling corridors that seemed, as they always had, and now as The Poet dreamed them, so endless, so filled, truly, with the pursuit of happiness, just around the corner, just within the next ajar doorway, just over the next cot in the orgy room of the dorm; the waters of the oval swimming pool in the subterranean depths of these heavenly baths sparkled with a cerulean blue fire, as the shades of naked males, lunging out of the inferno of the billowing steam room, sliced its cool surface as they plunged into its deeps—Yes, as The Poet as see-er saw, the sacred baths, all filled now and alive again with the roseate faces and bodies of all who had ever entered its doors through all the years of its existence—They were all there, all the spirits of the past, the known and the unknown, the old and the young, the fat and the skinny and the ugly and all those others so incredibly beautiful as to take the breath away; yes, they were all there again, and they were smiling, they were smiling at each other with smiles of anticipation, wrapped in their pristine bath towels the color of clouds, and they were smiling and nodding at each other as they passed in the long rosy corridors, light the color of flesh after a good love-making, light the color of flesh after the intense heat of the steam room, the sauna; and they smiled and nodded at The Poet and many were spirits The Poet had known, as lovers, as friends, as tricks, as members of ACT UP.

"O come back! Come back!" he shouted, in the ages-old cry of the poet, acutely aware of the perishing of things, as he stood now in the middle of the empty sidewalk holding a book and a blossom above his head in front of what was now called The Evergreen Mart but which was transformed in his Mind's Eye into the Old Everard Baths, while early morning passersby, mostly immigrant Asians on their way to open their shops along the street, stared at him curiously.

"O come back!" he begged. "Let it be as it was! O let it!"

And Big Sister, through the sparrow's beak of Asmaralda, twittered in his ear:

> Hoof and horn
> Hoof and horn
> All that dies
> Will be reborn.
>
> Corn and grain
> Corn and grain
> All that falls
> Will rise again.

And it was as it was, for it was over, and they waved to him, they waved and waved; oh, they were all there again—all the dead he had loved, all the dead writers he had read and loved, and the faces of so many he didn't know, but loved the same, thousands and tens of thousands; they were all smiling and nodding silently and looked so alive and healthy, for it was over, over, and the only sound was the jingle of cubicle and locker keys on all their ankles, tinkling like wind chimes, and they waved and waved, and The Poet waved back . . . And it was over, and they marched out of the baths and out into West 28th Street, where the windows of the wholesale florists, as they had been for a hundred years or more, were crammed to bursting with the early spring flowers of May, for it was over, and the spirits from the baths poured down West 28th, heading for 5th Avenue, where they marched, even more numerous than in the Pride marches, fifty abreast in row after row as far as the eye could see down the avenue in the direction of the Washington Square Arch, where Edna St. Vincent Millay and other poets and artists, as The Poet had read, one New Year's Eve so long ago had climbed to the top and waved a banner of poetic victory of the right to be different; the spectral marchers now shaking and smacking tambourines and blowing whistles, heading back to the homeland, the old familiar mile-square turf of the Queer Nation: Greenwich Village, "declared free and independent" by Millay and the others that long-ago night; thousands and thousands of them passing under the Arch and scattering under the trees of Washington Square, dancing and shouting and singing, beating their tambourines and blowing their whistles, arms about each other or holding hands, laughing and kissing and laughing and dancing under the green trees of springtime Washington Square, for it was over; and there, under the trees on the grass, were the children, playing in the spattered sunlight through the leaves; they ran about and threw balls and their mothers and fathers, all free now, all free of it all, sit quietly on the grass, smiling, watching them; the hemophiliacs were there, and those who'd been given infected blood in transfusions, all, all children and youths and grown men and women, the sons and daughters and mothers and fathers, of all ages, shapes and sizes, and the gay and the straight and the not so gay and the not so straight, all of the Pansexual Nation were there; for it was over, and all were there, under the trees in the spangled light, for it was over, over . . . and the park was now so crowded they spilled out into the surrounding streets of Washington Square East, and West, and South, and North, for it was over, dancing and singing in the shadow of New York University and in the row of brick Federal-style houses on Washington Square North and dancing near the house where Henry James was born, just off the Square, and dancing in the yellow brick light of Judson Memorial Church to the south . . . dancing and dancing in and out among the trees, for it was over, it was over at long last, all the dark and dread and fear-numbing days were over and . . .

Asmaralda who, still a sparrow, had been flying in circles around The Poet's head all this while, now flew down and pecked at his left ear again. The Poet stood flat-footed in the middle of the sidewalk, feeling like he did when he woke from a terrific dream, where he always felt so incredibly wonderful he wanted to go back to sleep instantly and dream it some more. But, rubbing his eyes, he saw now where he was: in the middle of West 28th Street just off Broadway, with its shabby rows of 19th-century tenements and storefronts looking even more vividly shabby in the unblinking light of the sun lifting over their rooftops, and before him the gutted, shabby corpse of the old Everard Baths, sprawled solidly once again now on solid Manhattan rock, from which all the ghosts of his vision had once again vanished.

"Whatever has possessed me?" he asked aloud, scratching his left ear as if a mosquito had bitten him. He saw a speck of blood on his fingertip and hit the side of his head, like a swimmer shaking water from his ear.

No, he saw, glumly, it was not over. It was as it was. The Everard was still long gone, with all its phantoms. The Plague was still very much here. All the dead were dead. And The Cardinal, The Cardinal was still very much alive.

He lay the gladiola blossom on the dusty worn tiles of the old baths' front step, then slipped the paperback novel back into his knapsack and once more hoisted the pack onto his shoulders. Retracing his steps, he crossed Broadway again a half block east, then continued on West 28th til he came to 5th Avenue where, again checking his watch, he quickened his pace, seeing The Demo would be starting in half an hour. He made a left and continued north up 5th to The Cathedral, still some twenty blocks away.

Already, on either side of the street, he saw more straggling bands of people in ever-increasing numbers marching up, in the opposite direction of the ghostly hordes in his vision, from Chelsea and the Village, carrying signs and banners, and heading in the same direction as he was.

After pecking Peter on the ear a second time to wake him, Asmaralda flew north over the rooftops of the West Side on *her* way to The Cathedral and the Sunday morning Demo, flying higher and higher the further uptown she went, to avoid hitting the midtown skyscrapers.

A pearl-colored stretch limo purred up in front of The Cathedral, and out of its rear stepped The Mayor himself, his rubbery features grinning broadly, his trademark bushy red hair aflame in the mid-morning sunlight. He flashed A-OK signs in response to the boos and hisses of those activists already gathered behind the police lines near the front steps, before his bodyguards whisked him up the steps and in a side door off the main vestibule (a door, unbeknownst to them, The Cardinal's own bodyguards would be using, as an emergency exit, in little more than an hour) that led to the rear of the building and to the sacristy.

And as Asmaralda wings her way north, perhaps it is time to mention here that her street sisters who, seeing her always clutching her grimy burlap bag whenever she left Avenue D, saw her, as her own corporeal self, of course, only as one of themselves, were wary of her squatting with whites (they didn't of course know, as Asmaralda knew—intuited, really—that Deirdre was part black). They saw her as probably being used as an "Aunt Jemima" (they might have said a "magical black mammy," had they known of her Big Sister powers), used to serve and slave for the white folks, the archetypical fat black mammy in white history and buried in the white (imperialist, some would say) unconscious, the one a lot of white gay males regularly dream of—including Peter The Poet: the Hattie McDaniel of *Gone With the Wind,* feeding and comforting and caring for whites at the neglect of herself and her own.

They could not know that Asmaralda did look after her own: several times a week she visited, invisibly, the children with AIDS ward in Harlem

Hospital and a similar ward in Lincoln Hospital in the South Bronx, the hospital where she herself had been taken after being born on the sidewalk: she was the child cradler in invisible arms; she was the crooner of lullabies heard only in their ears.

She also visited mothers with AIDS in those same hospital wards; she was the cool but unseen hand on the sweating brow; she was the hand in the hand of the AIDS-thin woman sick, too, with worry about her approaching death and what was going to become of her kids.

She took "refreshments," as she called them, to the children and women in these wards, potions, really, that she brewed on her little sterno stove at the top of the house on Avenue D, and that seemed to help them.

She went through the walls of the crack houses in Alphabet City, East Harlem, Bed-Stuy, and hugged the women who were mothers, and hugged the mothers on Welfare with kids who sold crack to make ends meet; she caressed them and comforted them; she gave them a momentary steadiness; she whispered love poems and love songs in their ears, "Love and respect yourself/As I love and respect you . . . /Be woman-strong/Be woman-brave . . ." and "Get your sweet ass to Narcotics Anonymous . . ."

She also slipped magic powders—the recipes of combinations of carefully ground herbs whispered in her ear in dreams by Big Sister—surreptitiously into Deirdre's drinking water bucket, that Peter The Poet left outside Deirdre's door each morning; slipped such powders, too, into the drinks of other women at women's bars, to fend off, as Big Sister, in dream-talk, put it, "not only the rigor mortis of booze but the rigor mortis of a man-made Gawd in a man-made world."

And finally, as we know, being more of a trickster than he himself, she left a jar of specially brewed tea outside Tom's door each morning, that also helped to keep his body free of intruders, just as she kept the house free of intruders from off the streets.

And, of course, she used these Big Sister powers sparingly, and only for good—like the time she gave constipation for a week to the five U.S. Supreme Court judges who voted it legal to enter and arrest citizens in their bedrooms while they're having sex the State does not like, constipation that no laxative or enema could cure.

And when she wasn't busy with such as that, she took care of herself, too. She didn't smoke, and, as has been said, she didn't drink or drug, just as the others in her house didn't either. If there was a good movie in town, she moved invisibly through the lobby doors, snatching several boxes of Raisinettes from the candy counter on the way, and floated into the theater, unseen by any of the staff, especially the ticket taker (she'd never bought a movie ticket since Big Sister's first visitation).

Occasionally, she would help herself to a double-dip ice cream cone at the Häagen-Dazs Ice Cream Shop on MacDougal Street in the Village, while the teen-aged help, in their red caps and aprons, stood goggle-eyed as the ice cream dipper moved of its own accord in mid-air, scooping up those two extra large scoops of deep-deep chocolate and slapping them on a sugar cone, the cone also balancing itself magically in mid-air; then the whole shebang flying out the door in a twinkling and disappearing up the street, while the help stared after, open-mouthed.

Or she sat quietly in a corner in bars or lofts or at the end of a West Street pier to listen carefully wherever women gathered to sing their songs, to speak their poems. She was everywhere and anywhere; she played it all across the board.

Such was Asmaralda's invisible life, that her street sisters could not know of, nor Tom nor Peter nor Deirdre know of, nor anyone at all (save for Big Sister, who kept her in her eye), except that all who came in contact with her were in some way touched by it, and changed.

At the very moment that Peter The Poet was turning onto 5th Avenue and Asmaralda was flying ahead of him uptown, Tom The Trickster, having beforehand carefully rubbed a generous amount of the rosin he'd lifted from The Face It into his hands and into the toes and onto the soles of his Nikes, and having hurtled the high, spiked, wrought-iron fence as neatly as he hurtled a subway turnstile, was just beginning his ascent up the rear wall of The Chancellory on Madison Avenue, its gray stone so worn and pocked with age and the acidity of city air pollution it made for a very rough surface, like the coarsest sandpaper, which enabled him to get good handholds, A piece of cake, so far, he grinned to himself, as he now scampered so swiftly up the back wall as not to be noticed at all.

Meanwhile, at the same time that Tom was slithering, lizard-like, up the rear wall of The Chancellory, inside, The Cardinal, having finished his hearty breakfast, which would be his last meal, if The Poet's aim was on target, was making his way, accompanied by Brother Francis, from the dining room to the gloomy old gothic passageway that connected The Chancellory with The Cathedral, and which led directly to the sacristy where the specially select were already gathered for the vesting ceremony, which meant, with Brother Francis's assistance, he would soon be getting into his robes and vestments to say late morning mass.

Although Deirdre was light on her feet, walking for any distance, unlike Peter The Poet, was not her forte, so she scrimped and saved from the little she got from Welfare, and did without, in order to take the bus or subway whenever she had to, as now, that morning, as she set off in the opposite direction of that taken by Peter and, earlier, by Tom The Trickster. Heading south on Avenue D to Gustave Hartman Square, she slowly, deliberately made her way to the crosstown bus stop on East Houston Street, a bus that would take her to the West Village and to Kitty's tiny, rent-controlled hole-in-the-wall apartment on Prince Street, near MacDougal.

The Latino men gathered at the curb, mouths, as always, agape whenever they saw her, their dark eyes swaying with her hips as they watched her move down the block. They called her "*La Grandita*"—Big Mama. Among themselves they considered her one of the wonders of Alphabet City.

As the bus doors hissed open, Deirdre hauled herself aboard, enjoying, as always, even more than her admiring Latino neighbors, the heft of herself, her Goddess-given solidity pulling up from gravity. Since it was Sunday and still pretty early, the bus was not very crowded. She chose a seat in the middle of the bus, the hard plastic cracking and snapping as she lowered herself, her ample girth spilling over both empty seats so that she, in effect, got two seats for the price of one, a bargain that never failed to please her. She liked to meditate while riding on buses and subways, and today she especially wished to continue her communion with The Goddess, as she had been doing back on Avenue D, because of the "duty," as she thought of it, that lay before her that morning at The Cathedral.

She was, unlike The Poet as he hurried up 5th Avenue, still feeling a determined calm, thanks to the forked magic of Asmaralda's fingers and the powdered herbs she pinched into Deirdre's water bucket that morning.

But suddenly two seats directly in front of her came the disconcertingly loud music of a Loudmouth blaster turned up at full volume, resting on the slim shoulder of a youth who had gotten on at Avenue B, thus making meditation all but impossible.

"I'm extremely heterosexual—not bisexual!" roared from the dual speakers, rap lyrics Peter The Poet would've recognized as by Tight A, and had he been there would've quoted Margaret Mead's "extreme heterosexuality is a perversion . . ."

Deirdre began a slow burn. Although she put up with, as said earlier, the male merengue rhythms perpetually blasting up from the cars beneath her windows on Avenue D, the one sound that irritated her more than any other, except for maybe a turned up Sony Walkman with its tinny, hissing beat, was a "ghetto blaster" blasting at high volume, distracting her from her meditations. At such moments, she, who did not believe in capital punishment, thought the electric chair should be reserved only for such inconsiderates who poisoned the very airwaves around them.

The youth, oblivious to the ears of the other

100

passengers, not to mention to the NO RADIO/ TAPE DECK PLAYING sign over the indifferent bus driver's head, slumped in his seat, the deafening music playing on.

Had The Poet been there, he could have also identified these rap lyrics as being by rapster Big Papa Pain:

> The Big Papa LAW
> Is anti-queer
> Now get that straight
> Right in your ear . . .

and which were so loud they could be heard over the bus's engine.

The Poet would have also recognized the youth as the very same one he'd spotted earlier on Avenue D, whose blaster had been playing similar rap lyrics.

Hearing the lyrics herself now, Deirdre began a faster burn. She prayed to The Goddess that some alternative, and benevolent, electronics firm (if only she and other women had the capital to do it!) would invent a battery-powered electronic gadget, a zapper, that a citizen could carry hidden in his or her pocket or bag that would, with the press of a secret button, zap off any blaster playing anti-gay or anti-woman lyrics (Peter The Poet certainly could have used one earlier that morning!), or as now when Deirdre was trapped in a bus, sitting close to someone blasting his Loudmouth, to simply press the pocket zapper to silence it, as a blow, in both cases, against ear pollution, *and* The Big Papa law.

The electric chair candidate in this case was now jiggling spastically in his seat to Big Papa Pain.

101

"One can at least take pleasure in the fact that he's going slowly deaf," drawled Deirdre to herself, with some satisfaction, "Not that he wasn't deaf to begin with," and then a smile creased her broad and generous features as an idea hit her: "Why not get in a few practice licks before the main event?" she figured.

She waited til the bus got to West Broadway, two blocks before her stop at MacDougal, then she pulled herself out of her seat and, all her bulk quivering in righteous indignation (after all, she *had* been deprived of precious meditation time), she bent over the youth in a sparring posture, fists clenched, just as June "The Left Hooker" Plizinsky had taught her at The Women's Martial Arts Center, shouting at the top of her capacious lungs so that even the youth, over the loudness of the music gradually taking away his hearing, heard her loud and clear: "TURN OFF THAT GODDESS-DAMNED MUSIC!"

That even got the apathetic bus driver's attention, as he stared at her in the rearview mirror.

The youth, seeing those massive fists, not to mention those massive shoulders and tits looming over him like The Giant Goddess Herself— and, in her muu-muu, a great orange one at that—shrank away wild-eyed into the corner of his seat, sniveling, "Whyn'tcha pick on somebody yer own size, man."

At this, Deirdre The Rad Dyke threw back her shoulders and shook with laughter, laughter louder even than the Loudmouth blaster. She yanked the cord to signal her stop and as she exited through the rear door, the bus driver continuing to watch her curiously as she got herself around sideways to step down, her shoulders were still shaking.

And as she walked down the street, she stepped

with a certain proud and confident swagger. She held her head high. She felt even larger. She felt larger than life.

She didn't get in her practice punch, after all, but she felt even more certain about what she planned to do at The Demo, and for that she thanked The Goddess, as she turned south on MacDougal to Prince Street and her beloved Kitty whom she was just busting to tell all about her adventure on the crosstown bus.

Kitty was a tough little nut from Brooklyn. And "little" she was, at four foot two and weighing less than 90 pounds. She and Deirdre drew stares and behind-the-hand titters wherever they went. But it didn't bother either of them. If someone were foolish enough to make a wisecrack, like the tired old one about Kitty looking like The Depression and Deirdre looking like the one who caused it, he or she soon knew the labrys-sharp edge of Kitty's tongue.

Kitty loved Deirdre's fat as much as Deirdre did herself. She called her "my mountain" (and in the throes of ecstasy "my mountain flower"), and in bed loved to climb up Deirdre's massive, high-domed belly and roll down it. It was a game they called "Dyke-on-the-Mountain."

Kitty wasn't happy about Deirdre squatting in an abandoned tenement, but her apartment was indeed as tiny as herself and would have been impossible with two living there, especially with someone the size of Deirdre. There was a tiny front room and cooking alcove, an equally tiny bath (Deirdre, to accommodate her haunches, had to ride the toilet seat side saddle, which caused them no end of amusement), but she never felt cramped in it, except when her beloved Deirdre

103

was there. Even so, she loved the way Deirdre filled the space, she loved having to climb over or around her, never of course missing an opportunity to brush against those succulent, giant, women-only breasts or thighs—or, for that matter, "the Great Smoky Mountains," as she called them, of Deirdre's mountainous buttocks.

The air of the apartment was filled with the subtle but delectable aroma of a chive omelette Kitty was cooking for their Sunday morning breakfast at a very low flame on the two-burner gas stove—a tea kettle steamed on the other burner. She had snipped fresh chives earlier from her tiny planter of an herb garden that sat in the one window where the morning sun came in.

The delicious fragrance of the omelette was not enough, however, to override the odor of her cats, who lay in a comfortable tangle on the unmade convertible sofa bed, which just about filled the front room. Kitty, like any other self-respecting lesbian, had cats—four in fact—Eartha Kitt, Katharine Hepburn, and Cagney and Lacey (she and Deirdre were avid TV and late night movie buffs)—so that her little apartment was always filled with fur balls and the fishiest smell of cheap cat food (on a computer clerk's salary, that was all she could afford), not to mention the ammoniac reek of cat pee from the kitty litter box under the sink, even though she emptied the box into a plastic bag and dumped the bag in the garbage cans out front each and every day.

She was preparing the greens for a salad (in honor of The Jolly Green Goddess, they ate salads at *every* meal) when she heard Deirdre's knock, two quick raps followed by a heavier one—their signal. They were salad greens that she and Deirdre had picked in Central Park the day before in a little shady ravine they'd discovered some-

104

time back, down off The Ramble near West 72nd Street (where they occasionally spotted Peter The Poet, unbeknownst to him, frisking satyr-like with other lads under the sunlit-dappled shade of the trees and bushes; and once or twice they came upon Asmaralda, in the shadiest glades, bent over and stuffing her burlap bag with what she shyly called "simples"). They'd brought home bunches of the first tender dandelion leaves (rich with iron) and shoots of violet leaves (loaded with Vitamin C), and a basket of wild mushrooms with their pungent taste of the earth (they'd taken the mushroom book along just to be on the safe side).

The moment Kitty unchained and unlocked the various locks on her door and let Deirdre in, she, as always, grabbed a kitchen chair and bounding up on it, agile as one of her cats, who all leapt off the sofa bed and began rubbing themselves around Deirdre's ankles, sank her head on Deirdre's breast and hugged and hugged her beloved, her small arms barely encircling that generous bosom.

And Deirdre, as always, for Kitty was a very good cook, one of those who could whip up a tasty meal out of nothing, sniffed the air and then rolling her eyes toward the freshly washed greens in the sink, in a mock-stage voice, not unlike Sophie Tucker's, made her usual little jape about Kitty's spare cuisine: "I fatten on your love, my love, most certainly not on your grub."

And Kitty, as always, elbowed her in the gut, grinning and saying in equally mock complaint, "Oh *you!*"

"But oh! let me tell you!" exclaimed Deirdre breathlessly, and after she told Kitty her story of the incident on the bus and, when she ended with the offending youth's "Whyn'tcha pick on somebody yer own size, man," Kitty clapped her hands

and laughed merrily, kissing her Deirdre again
and again and telling her how proud she was of
her; then she rushed to the sofa bed and pulled
out from under it a sign taller than she was that
she'd made the night before for The Demo, which
read in big "clit-pink," as she called it, block letters:

> STOP VIOLENCE
> AGAINST LESBIANS
> AND ALL WOMEN
> STOP THE CHURCH!!!

of which Deirdre heartily approved.

Having thoroughly indoctrinated Kitty to the
ways of The Goddess—no caffeine, no nicotine,
and certainly no booze, no other drugs—they
sipped lemon grass tea, and then the omelette
was ready, and Kitty served that along with the
salad, sprinkling the latter with a bit of safflower
oil and vinegar just the way Deirdre liked it.

After they'd finished eating, Deirdre checked
her Timex and seeing they still had a little time
before having to set out for The Cathedral, took
Kitty's small hand in her larger one and gave her
the wink, nodding her head pointedly toward the
sofa bed, which Kitty, with calculated fore-
thought, as always, hadn't folded away that
morning.

"Wanna play Dyke-on-the-Mountain?" Deirdre
whispered.

Kitty shot back a wickedly impish grin.

"Is The Cardinal a homophobic sexist pig?"

Then, nuzzling up to Deirdre's enormous left
nipple, she began to hymn one of their secret, intimate hymns of thanksgiving to The Goddess:
"Thanks for the Mammaries."

"Ummmm," murmured Deirdre dreamily, folding Kitty in her arms so that Kitty all but disappeared in her great folds of flesh, forgetting for the moment, as she and Kitty repaired to the bed, the cats scattering in all directions, and in the long luxurious moments of "sipping at the honeypot" that followed, the date she had made with herself with The Cardinal an hour or so hence.

At that very moment, The Cardinal, oblivious, of course, to any such appointment, paused in the dark passage as Brother Francis hurried forward and, with a cringing bow, swung open the massive door of the sacristy.

His Excellency, a faint smile of anticipation parting his thin, pallid lips, swept past him into the low-vaulted room, dispensing as he went hasty signs of the cross left and right to the specially invited clergy and political dignitaries lined up against the far wall.

At the very same time that The Cardinal was entering his sacristy and Deirdre and Kitty were playing "Dyke-on-the-Mountain," Skint The Skinhead was taking a piss. He loved looking at his "piece," as he called it, as much as Deirdre The Rad Dyke loved looking at her fat. Although the two had never met, had he met her he would've probably spat in her face. Standing buck naked, spread leg, he eyed his "piece," never tiring of it: uncut, skin peeled back, revealing that bulbous glossy red head out of the slit of which a hard, thick yellow stream splattered into the cracked, filthy toilet bowl in the equally filthy bathroom of his apartment on Avenue A. In his left pierced earlobe was a small silver swastika earring; on his rather muscular upper right bicep was a tat-

107

too of the face of Hitler, box mustache and all, and under it in Nazi-red letters (Skint's favorite color): WHERE ARE YOU NOW THAT WE NEED YOU? This always got a big laugh, especially when he flexed it, from the newcomers to The Klub over on Avenue C ("the Klub" meant also as in a club to club with), a punk rock biker's hangout for other skinheads, where Skint was a bouncer.

He had been born and reared on Avenue A, in fact not many doors away on this same block, near East 5th Street: blue collar Polish-Irish Catholic. His father, Stan, one of those first-generation American-Poles who, on their days off, used to stand in front of the saloons on Saint Mark's Place, jawing with their worker pals in Polish, all of them wearing old wide pinstripe suit coats with wide lapels, had worked for years in a foundry out in Long Island City; while Skint's mother, a failed novitiate—she had been booted out of the nunnery after less than a year for forming what her Mother Superior had termed "a particular friendship" with another equally nubile novitiate, a secret she swore she'd carry to her grave, "May God forgive me"—stayed home all day in their cramped fifth floor walkup raising nine kids, the youngest of which was Skint.

Like The Cardinal, whom he admired tremendously, even though he himself was a "lapsed Catholic," as they say, Skint had had a thorough early religious education, going first to parochial school, Saint Stanislaus's, over on East 8th Street, then on to the all-boys La Salle Academy which was also on the Lower East Side, before he dropped out in his sophomore year, the year his father died, no longer able "ta' take da' shit anymore," as he phrased it.

"Da' shit" had started quite early. Skint was street-smart but school *slow;* he was fast, though, with the lip, which got him in trouble at school from the start. Many a crack had he gotten on the head from the sharp edge of the good sisters' rulers at Saint Stanislaus's—his now-shaved skull revealed the numerous nicks and scars; many a hiding had he gotten on his bare behind from the thick leather belt of a certain good brother at La Salle (and many a punch in the face did many a smaller or brainier kid get in the schoolyard at recess or in the gym, as a result). And when the notes from school arrived home in the mail, Skint's old man was quick with his hands, especially when he'd had a few, knocking Skint flat, til one day he noticed Skint was a good two heads taller than himself and instead of laying him out, he did the prudent thing: he took off up to Stosh's Saloon on Saint Mark's and knocked down quite a few more than usual.

Skint admired The Cardinal because, like Peter The Poet, always listening to him when he appeared on TV, he understood that The Cardinal was just as "anti-fag" as he was and saw The Cardinal and himself as "*good* terrorists, keepin' da' degenerates down."

Skint The Skinhead was "anti" a lot of things, but he was mainly "anti-fag." It was one of the big reasons he wanted to be at The Demo at The Cathedral that morning. He'd seen Tom The Trickster several times on TV talking for ACT UP and recognized him around the neighborhood, but Tom always managed to outrun him. Skint figured he'd be there. If Deirdre The Rad Dyke wanted to sock The Cardinal in the worst way, Skint The Skinhead couldn't wait to get his hands on Tom The Trickster, or "any a' dem diseased faggots," for that matter.

It was "da' fags," he believed, who started wrecking *his* neighborhood in the first place (followed later "by da' Wall Street yuppies"), coming in with their "la-de-la" gentrification, not to mention "their fuckin' AIDS," and driving out respectable working-class old-timey families like his: solid, working-class Polish-Irish Catholics ("da' spics and niggers" didn't of course "count"). People like his father, mercifully in his coffin before the old neighborhood changed, laid out in his Sunday dark blue pinstripe with the wide lapels, "dead of the cigs and the booze and a life of back-breakin' toil," as Skint's Irish mother put it.

Finally, when their building had been bought by "a bunch a' cocksuckin' faggots ta' pretty it up, and up da' rents," to use Skint's own words, she'd been forced to move in with her life-long friend, the widow Rafferty, the very same, The Cardinal's head housekeeper and cook, further down the Avenue. Skint was awful surprised at how quick his mother got over not only his old man's death but having to move "downtown," even though Mrs. Rafferty had only one bedroom and she and his mother had to sleep in the same bed. In spite of that, his mother never seemed happier. She and "Mrs. R.," as his mother called her, went to early mass together every morning at Saint Bridget's, before "Mrs. R." took the subway uptown to The Chancellory and her job, and in fact at all other times they seemed inseparable, going everywhere together, like "dey was reg'lar siamese twins," as the neighbors put it.

Like most American sons ("Sentimentality is the obverse of brutality," as Peter The Poet always said to impress people, paraphrasing Jung), Skint had a soft spot in his heart for "his ma." So he was secretly glad she was getting along OK, and had "Mrs. R." for company. He went to see her as often as he could, always bringing her a little something: a loaf of Wonder Bread or a bag of tomatoes or those dark purple plums she especially liked, pinching whatever he could, like Tom The Trickster, except, unlike Tom, who stole only from out-and-out "'phobes," Skint boosted from shops he knew were either "fag-owned" or where the clerks "*looked* faggy." Hence, like Tom, that gave him wide latitude all over the East Village.

He gave his "piece" a good shake—one, two, three—"more'n three," as the boys used to say at La Salle, "and yer jerkin' off," kidstuff today to Skint, but even so he never forgot it and never shook it more than three times. Peeling down the skin—had Peter The Poet (whom Skint'd also never met but if he had he would've "punched da' fag out") been there, he would have, admiringly, called such a shrivelly long foreskin "lace curtains"—Skint returned to the dark bedroom, dark because, like The Poet's, the shadeless, curtainless windows were so grimy, even when the sun was out, as now, very little light leaked in.

In the gloom, however, his shaved skull gleamed (he was blonde and blue-eyed and could've passed in the Nazi era for one of Hitler's "pure Aryan dream children"—except for his Polish blood, of course). Also just visible was a sagging king-sized mattress, from his mother's and father's bed from the old apartment, which filled up most of the floor, and where barely discernible on it, tangled in dirty sheets the color of the sidewalks below, a naked leg and breast exposed, sprawled Corkie, Skint's "ole lady."

"Gitcher tail outa' that sack," he snarled. "We gotta git up ta' da' fuckin' cathedral."

"Ummm," breathed Corkie sleepily, turning, so that her other bare breast slipped out of the sheet. She was small, but not as small as Deirdre's Kitty, and very, very pale, with skin that seemed never to have seen sunlight.

"What's wit'chou, ya' got religion all of a sudden?" she murmured.

"It's dat fag demo—I got some business up 'dere . . ."

Skint was staring at her tits. If he couldn't get enough of staring at his cock, he certainly couldn't get enough of staring at Corkie's tits. He walked up on the mattress and planted a foot wide either side her hips, straddling her like the picture of an old colossus he'd seen in a history book at school, and peering down at her, fondling his "piece," which was ready to fire.

He could smell her.

"What 'business' ya' talkin' about?" she whined sleepily. "Whatcha' got up yer sleeve now?"

God, he loved the smell of pussy. He loved the taste. He couldn't ever get enough of it. And Corkie was one juicy pussy. He clutched himself harder, almost fully up now just thinking about Corkie's cooz.

She lifted her head off the mattress.

"I see ya' got some 'business' on yer mind right now," she drawled, and whipped the sheet aside and spread her legs wide.

Although she tried to hide it, as always, seeing that "piece," there was a look of fright in her flat, dark eyes. Even so, she forced a grin and stretched her arms up to reach for him.

"You wanna' pork yer Cork? Huh? Is that what you want?"

If nothing else, Corkie knew her place.

For answer he dropped on top of her, then buried his face hungrily between her thighs, "scarfin' away like it's Da' Last Supper," he thought to himself, grinning at his blasphemy, then biting her labia in tiny nips. As she squealed, as always, in pleasure and pain, he reared up on her and, as usual, without warning, rammed his cock deep in

112

up to the pubes, so that she screamed louder, as she always did, which only excited him more, making him ram harder and harder.

Fucking for Skint The Skinhead was not much different from rape.

In his black leather motorcyclist's cap, snug black leather jacket, black T-shirt with huge white death's skull and AIDS KILLS FAGS DEAD emblazoned across the chest, tight black leather form-fitting pants that showed his monstrous endowment off to full advantage, and, of course, black leather jackboots with steel safety tips the better to kick with, Skint The Skinhead was dressed to face the day. As he strutted out the front door of the tenement, with surly-faced Corkie dragging behind (she'd rather have stayed home and smoked dope, but she knew better than to complain), his silver swastika earring glistened as it caught the now-full morning sunlight slanting down over Avenue A.

At first glance, he looked every inch the lean, mean biker. There was only one thing missing: the shiny black Harley-Davidson itself chained up outside his doorstep.

One of Skint's biggest humiliations, and there were, to his mind, many, was that he didn't make enough money at The Klub to buy a 'cycle and thus had to ride the buses and subways in his motorcycle gear "like da' rest a' da' assholes," as he had to now as he and Corkie headed toward the Astor Place subway station, the same station, unbeknownst of course to Skint, that Tom The Trickster had departed from several hours earlier for his climb up The Cathedral.

Most of the people on the street now were on their way to late mass (as were, each in his or her own way, our cast of characters as they made their separate ways to The Cathedral), Latinos mostly, women mostly walking with little girls and boys, all in their Sunday best. Whenever Skint passed a "spic" or a "nigger," as now, he erased them, they became invisible in his eyes— "rubbed out" by an act of his will. There weren't as many "yids" left on the Lower East Side, not as many as when he was a kid, he thanked God; most of them now were living over in Crown Heights in Brooklyn or out in Queens, so it was mainly the Latinos and blacks he had to erase now—and most certainly "da' fags, dykes, and other uppity, pushy cunts that don't know der place."

That, of course, in Alphabet City, left very few faces he had to bother with.

He gave Corkie a hard smack on the behind, to get her moving.

In her revival mini, as black as Skint's jackboots, which *just* exposed the bottoms of her firmly rounded ass-cheeks—Skint wouldn't let her wear panties—she smiled up at him, gratefully.

A slap from Skint was a love-tap to her.

As they passed the cemetery on East 3rd Street, heading toward 2nd Avenue, all of Skint's senses became instantly alert, his nose quivering like a mastiff on the scent, as a guy, maybe in his early twenties, walked hurriedly towards them, obviously also heading for The Demo, Skint figured, what with his dozen or so "SILENCE = DEATH" buttons with their pink triangles on a black background down the front of his ACT UP T-shirt. Skint could feel all his skin prickle and every hair on his body stiffen, the way he figured a dog must feel when he sniffs a cat or a strange human in the vicinity (and Skint, like a watchdog, considered all of Alphabet City his home turf).

Just as the youth passed Skint, his eyes, by-passing the T-shirt's message, momentarily dropping to admire the enormous bulge in Skint's skin-tight leather crotch ("Every faggot loves a fascist," as Peter The Poet was fond of saying, paraphrasing Plath), Skint, without a word, without changing expression or missing a step, shot out his long, powerful right arm, the one with the Hitler tattoo, and just as he did when getting rid of an unwanted customer, an "alien" as he called them, at The Klub, slammed the young man smack in the jaw.

"Dat's one for Da' Cardinal," he growled, rubbing his knuckles briskly on one thigh of his leather trousers, not because he'd hurt them, it'd take more than a fag's glass jaw to do that, but in a gesture of "cleaning" them off. "Ya' never know where der mouths've bin," he muttered, his own mouth still tasting of where *it* had just recently been.

The young man, sitting knocked on his ass in the middle of the pavement, stared back wide-eyed, clumsily rubbing his chin, his head wobbling as if he were seeing stars.

Skint The Skinhead whipped out the can of "Nazi-red," as he proudly called it, Krylon spray paint (just as Peter The Poet had earlier, except Peter's, as stated, was of course lavender), and squatting, hurriedly sprayed the following in big letters, as he always did whenever he gave " a knuckle sandwich" to anyone who looked in the slightest way queer: FAG BASHED HEER GASS FAGS.

All the while, Corkie was staring off in the dis-

115

tance over the iron fence of the cemetery as if she were thinking of something else—and indeed she was: some breakfast—and said not a word.

She thoroughly understood she'd better not.

He slapped her on the ass again, as if he had to do this each time to get her started, and before they turned up 2nd Avenue, he quickly spray-painted on a mailbox in that red that so excited him: FUCK A DIKE MAKE A WOMMAN OF HERR.

"I'm hun-n-n-gry," whined Corkie.

"Yeah, me too, babe," said Skint, as he shoved his spray paint can in his jacket pocket and slapping her bottom once more, led the way up 2nd.

He swaggered along the street toward a take-out joint on the corner of East 4th and The Bowery that he knew was open on Sundays, swaggering like Deirdre The Rad Dyke did when she got off the bus after she'd confronted the youth and his noisy Loudmouth, except Skint The Skinhead strutted like that all the time.

The last time we left Tom The Trickster, he was scampering up the rear wall of The Chancellory on Madison Avenue, behind The Cathedral. At the very moment that Skint The Skinhead and Corkie were heading for a late take-out breakfast on *their* way to The Cathedral, Tom was hoisting one leg up over the eaves of The Chancellory roof and sliding himself up onto its tiles. Once bellydown now on the roof itself, he paused for the barest fraction of a second to see if he'd been observed and, noting that the only person in the vicinity at that moment was a homeless vagrant in rags taking a leak in a boutique doorway across Madison (the very same beggar, in fact, who'd thrust his paper cup in Tom's unseeing face earlier on the subway), he got himself around and began slithering along on his belly up the steeply pitched incline, feeling like he had suddenly become all snake.

There were numerous obstacles, however, that Tom had anticipated in his photos: Besides the highly ornate wrought-iron fretwork, decorative "fences" lining the roof peaks, and the myriad chimney pots leading to the massive fireplaces scattered below in the rooms of The Chancellory—The Cardinal did so love a glass of sherry and a chat with his dear friend The Mayor in front of a good fire—there was an enormous satellite TV dish that could pull in 150 stations anywhere on the globe, not to mention an elaborate network of AM, FM, and short wave and police band radio aerials and antennas (one direct to Radio Vatican itself)—The Cardinal didn't want to miss a single one of his countless appearances in The Media—plus of course an antenna to the radio-phone in The Mayor's limo—all strewn like metallic clotheslines to garrote you or like sharp metallic spikes to impale you, if you weren't careful. So, when Tom encountered an obstacle and had to rise up to gain a hand- or foothold to get around it, he crouched as low as he could—with his pack he looked very much the hunched-back monkey—til he wormed his way around it and could slip down on his belly once more, sink out of sight as much as possible, and continue to shimmy his way up the sharp ascent.

Occasionally, one of the gray slate tiles broke beneath his fingers—so far, he could see that The Cardinal really could use a *real* roofer up there!— and went clattering down the roof into a rain gutter. When that happened, he would freeze for a moment or two, listening, then, when he felt it was safe to proceed, would go on with his climb.

117

As he reached the peak of that particular section of roof that separated The Chancellory from The Cathedral, and gripped the copper flashing running along the ridge to haul himself up and over, he was mightily thankful he'd had the foresight to take those climbing lessons at The Face It a few blocks further south!

Momentarily straddling the summit, he surveyed what lay ahead: once he slid down the other side he would be on the roof of The Cathedral itself or, as he also knew from his photos, one of its many roofs, for what spread before him were the numerous side peaks leading to the main body of the church itself and to the main steeples at the front entrance over on the 5th Avenue side, roofs that were even more sharply pitched than the roof of The Chancellory and that he had to get over before he could reach the north steeple, his final goal.

He saw he had his work cut out for him.

He also saw the palms of his hands were so black with soot he could no longer see the white of the rosin he'd so generously smeared on them before starting his climb. Then, glancing down at himself, he observed that from the chest down he was already pitch-black from the accumulated century of grime on the slate tiles and could very well have been mistaken by anyone below for a chimney sweep as well as a roofer. Actually, it was good camouflage, he realized, and was grateful for the grime: it made him look part of the roof and thus harder to spot from the streets below.

He was high enough now that he could see a few people making their way far below along both 50th and 51st Streets, all heading in the direction of the front entrance to The Cathedral, and early mass. He saw no signs of any protesters yet.

Checking his Timex, he saw he was right on schedule, that he had just enough time to make it over the adjacent roofs and the main roof to his goal.

On the 51st Street side he spotted several police already putting in place along the sidewalk a few of the blue Police Department sawhorse barricades with DO NOT CROSS in big white letters, getting ready for The Demo they had been well aware of in advance, particularly with the secret information supplied to them by The Cardinal's own "God's eyes," not to mention The Mayor's and The Police Commissioner's own secret operatives.

On the 50th Street side he heard the clatter of hoofs and turning saw a number of cops on horseback riding towards 5th Avenue. One of the cops glanced up in the vicinity of the roof where Tom The Trickster was still perched. Tom wasn't sure if he'd been spotted or not, but he quickly pulled a hammer from his roofer's tool belt and began, naively perhaps, tapping away at the tiles, like any busy roofer on an emergency call.

When he saw the cop was no longer looking his way, and had ridden on with the others, he jammed the hammer back in its loop and slid down the far side of the roof on his behind, ready now to begin his ascent and his eventual climb over the roofs of The Cathedral itself, making his way to the towering steeple in the distance.

Directly far below the sharply pitched roof down which Tom The Trickster had just slid, The Cardinal, in his sacristy, was making a slow turn toward the massive mahogany chest of drawers where his vestments, carefully hand-laundered and ironed by Mrs. Rafferty herself, lay spread out flat and waiting on their beds of soft snowy tissue within the long, narrow drawers themselves.

Brother Francis, in his hunched, unobtrusive way, sprang silently forward to slide open the first drawer containing the alb, its white linen fragrant with roses (Mrs. Rafferty, or "Mrs. R.," as Skint's mother affectionately called her, was well aware of how much His Grace loved that scent) that subtly perfumed the waxy, airless odor of the low-ceilinged room.

Like Tom The Trickster, a master fare beater, if ever there was one, Skint The Skinhead never paid a subway fare, and neither did Corkie. But whereas Skint, making, as always, a big defiant show of it, vaulted over the turnstile on one hand, as he did now at the Astor Place subway station— the token booth clerk squawked through her intercom but Skint, as usual, paid her no mind— Corkie, small as a child, was able to hunker down and waddle through beneath the stile. Which was a safer route, too, for their take-out breakfast which Corkie clutched in its brown bag and which Skint had her carry, as he made her tote everything.

The train was crowded mainly with others heading for The Demo, most of them gripping hand-printed placards and posters, a number of which read KEEP YOUR HANDS OFF MY BODY and CURB YOUR DOGMA, and others that were job-printed signs, such as KNOW YOUR SCUM-BAGS.

As Skint The Skinhead entered the car, with Corkie in tow, he drew himself to his full height and glared around with a lordly sneer at the motley crowd of activists, as if he'd suddenly found himself in a place crawling with vermin. He felt threatened by the thickets of placards and posters on sticks and banners rolled up on poles that surrounded him, not to mention the hostile stares of those in his immediate vicinity, what with his swastika earring and AIDS KILLS FAGS DEAD T-shirt; but now like a watchdog outside his turf, he kept a quiet but wary eye.

If he'd had him a big-assed Harley-Davidson he wouldn't have to ride the subway with such scum.

There weren't any seats left but that never stopped Skint: he shoved aside a sleeping homeless man and vigorously wiggled his hips down to make room on either side for him and Corkie, then spreading his legs wide in a gesture of declaring the space his, pulled Corkie down beside him.

As she wedged herself into the tiny space he'd made for her, she opened the paper bag and handed him his take-out: black coffee and cherry danish for him; black coffee, loaded with six sugars, and a bagel and cream cheese, heavy on the grape jelly, for her.

As Skint chomped away hungrily on his danish (he ate everything, in his own words again, like "it was Da' Last Supper"), he noticed in the seat directly across from him what he took at first to be an enormously fat mother sitting with her tiny daughter, a child in fact almost as tiny as his very own Corkie. However, a scowl darkened his fair features, he stopped his chomping in mid-bite, his hackles rising as he saw that the two were holding hands and mooning over each other in a way no mother or daughter would ever do, or at least hardly ever do.

To top it off, the midget-sized one was clutching a sign taller than she was that read in big pink letters:

STOP VIOLENCE
AGAINST LESBIANS
AND ALL WOMEN
STOP THE CHURCH!!!

The Skinhead growled.

The pair were, of course, Deirdre and Kitty who had gotten on at the Spring Street station one stop before Astor Place and were now, after their own breakfast, etc., etc., heading uptown to The Demo. Evidently those earlier-mentioned 150 or so intimate womanly scents were still intoxicating them, for they were so enraptured with each other they paid not the slightest attention to the scowling Skint. He was, as indeed were most men to Deirdre and Kitty, just another invisible male, erased from their field of vision (but for different reasons than the ones Skint The Skinhead erased all people of color).

He would've loved to jump across the car and punch them both out (had he known that Deirdre was also part "nigger," not to mention part Cuban, he would, in his eyes, have been doubly justified in punching her out). He didn't believe in hitting women, except for "dykes that wasn't *real* chicks anyhow," and except of course for Corkie who wasn't really a woman to him, either, but more often than not "a bad li'l girl" that needed to be taken in hand.

Being a good American son, he would never, never, of course, punch his own mother out.

Still, the sheer size of Deirdre gave him pause. Had he known of her recent boxing lessons at The Women's Martial Arts Center, and their purpose, that might've made him hesitate even more.

Prudently, he decided he'd shout something at them as he was leaving the subway car.

It was just as well. There were two Guardian

Angels in their red berets on board, posting guard with their arms folded at either end of the car. But since one was black and the other Latino, Skint, of course, with his automatic erasure system, didn't notice them.

Instead, he elbowed Corkie, jerking his head across the aisle in the direction of Deirdre and Kitty. Corkie, blank-faced, as ever, the better to keep her thoughts to herself, having already noticed the two, wondered how they managed in bed, wondered indeed, as she peered over her cream cheese and jelly bagel at Kitty, what it would be like to get it on with someone her own size for once, even if she was a dyke.

These speculations, of course, she did not pass along to Skint.

Instead, over the wheels of the train, she muttered in Skint's ear loud enough for him to hear, "Da' little one looks like Da' Depression and da' other one looks like she caused it."

Skint snorted and began tearing again into what was left of his cherry danish and slurping it down with the last of his coffee. That was a good one. He'd have to remember to tell that one to the guys at The Klub.

It was just a very good thing for Corkie that Kitty was still so wrapped up in her Deirdre that she hadn't overheard Corkie's feeble attempt at humor, or, as stated before, with her labrys-sharp tongue, there would've been hell to pay.

Damned if at that instant—he was nothing if not persistent—that same beggar came through the door at the far end of the car who had rattled his paper cup in Tom The Trickster's face on his way uptown on an earlier Number 6 train and whom Tom had spotted taking a leak behind The Chancellory. He evidently rode back and forth on this route all day long! He had a hard time weaving his way through the crowded car but occasionally you could hear coins being dropped into his cup from these more empathetic passengers, some of whom looked like they could use a handout themselves. But when he got to Skint The Skinhead, Skint, who had just downed the last swallow of his coffee, crumpled up the paper cup it'd been in and, as the beggar shook his own cup under Skint's nose, jammed the squashed, and squishy, cup into the beggar's, muttering loud enough for those around to hear, "GET A JOB, YOU SCUMBAG!"

The closest Guardian Angel, the black youth with a single golden earring in his right pierced ear, narrowed his eyes at Skint, as the beggar staggered away, clutching Skint's soggy coffee cup in one hand and continuing to rattle his own cup in the faces of the other passengers.

The two Guardian Angels got off at 42nd Street and, after the doors closed and the train was on its way uptown again, as if the departure of the two were a signal, the door of the front of the car burst open and the same gang that had run through the car snatching gold chains left and right on the earlier train Tom The Trickster had been on, once more came dancing through the car, snaking their way agilely among the crowded straphangers, and once again ripping chains from the throats of all who were wearing them. As earlier, there were screams and cries of protest, except now several women batted out at the intruders with their furled banners and placards on sticks, but the gang of youths wasn't at all intimidated, treated it as a game, deftly dodging the make-do weapons, as they quickly, skillfully, went about their work.

Skint folded his muscular arms in their black leather across his equally muscular chest and, although he was wearing no gold (the only jewelry he ever wore was the silver swastika earring) he had a steely glint in his eye that said: *Don't fuck with me.*

Seeing those eyes, and seeing no gold, none of the gang did; they just danced their way by him.

Even though neither Deirdre nor Kitty, since they were just scraping along, had any gold chains to steal either, still, when the gang danced near them, their deft fingers darting everywhere, Deirdre stood up in all her massiveness, not to mention in her new-found courage, thanks to Big Sister via Asmaralda, and, shielding her Kitty behind her with her own gigantic behind, defied the gang to bother them—even though Kitty, all 85 pounds of her, was quite capable of standing up and giving them a tongue-lashing they'd never forget.

"She's *big!*" one of the gang sang out good-naturedly; "It's cool," another sang out, and they danced away from Deirdre and boogied in and out down the aisle, ducking swinging signs as they went, til they got to the end of the car where they exited out the rear door into the next car.

Deirdre lowered herself in her seat again and hugged her Kitty close, just as the train was pulling into the 51st Street station, their stop, and just about everybody else's as well. It was, of course, Skint The Skinhead's and Corkie's stop too, and as the car ground to a halt and the doors slid open, Skint grabbed Corkie by the back of the neck and reaching the nearest door before anyone else, he turned to shout out at Deirdre and Kitty, indeed to all the women in the car since he saw them all as "lesbos," shouting in capital letters the same way he spray-painted: "YOU FUCKIN' DYKES, WHYN'TCHA GET FUCKED BY A REAL MAN!" meaning, presumably, him-

125

self, and tightening his hold on Corkie's neck, he tore out of the car and across the platform to the exit gate where he slammed out and up the steps to the street—not exactly running, mind you, but not exactly walking, either.

Having ascended and then slid down the various side roofs on the north side of The Cathedral, Tom The Trickster, after first rubbing copious quantities of fresh rosin on his hands, now was making his way along the high ridge of the main beam, straddling the peak and inching his way along by gripping the tiles on either side and humping himself forward.

As he did so, he could see either side of him the traffic still moving in the side streets that flanked The Cathedral, with more and more squads of the blue and white police cars and vans and dark police prison buses with wire guards in the windows parked along the curbs. But up front at the entrance to The Cathedral, he could hear no traffic, so he figured the cops must have closed off that part of 5th Avenue already.

He could also just see, on both streets running alongside The Cathedral, the tops of the new-budding trees, and seeing them from so high up filled him with the excitement of changes. Unlike The Poet, who really did believe his assassination of The Cardinal would change things, Tom The Trickster, along with many members of ACT UP, had no illusions that The Demo to STOP THE CHURCH would change The Church's position on *anything*. But it would show, Tom was convinced, that there were no longer any barriers. It would show, to those with eyes, who the truly violent were.

Since he still had half the main roof to cross and his vision was blocked by the stone balustrade atop the facade of the building, he heard rather than saw a growing clamor in front of The Cathedral; now and then snatches of shouts and chanting floated up to his ears, but much of it was so indistinct as yet from that distance, he couldn't quite make it out.

"YOU SAY CRACK UP! WE SAY ACT UP!" came across loud and clear, however.

Amid the chants, he could hear now the increasing clatter of hoofbeats on asphalt all around The Cathedral.

He grinned, looking in all his sootiness like a homeless person suddenly lifted atop the world, envisioning it all as a vast success, no matter the outcome.

Finally, he reached the end of the high ridge beam of the main peak and, still concealed by the balustrade atop the facade, slid down the north side of the main roof to the base of the steeple itself. Once there, he slipped off his pack and leaned against the rough stones, catching his breath again and grinning with satisfaction: the hardest part was over and, best of all, nobody had spotted him. Now all he had to do was wait. He wouldn't want to spring his trick before the right dramatic moment. No, everything was going according to plan. And like the beggar on the subway, whom he'd not noticed, Tom The Trickster understood the importance of patience.

He checked his watch. He knew from the anonymous messages left on ACT UP's answering machine by someone mimicking The Cardinal's voice, that he had another 45 minutes before The Cardinal delivered his homily and the mass ended; then, the main event of The Demo, as far

127

as he was concerned, would be set to begin. Suddenly famished, he unzipped his pack and pulled out the plastic bag of dried mixed fruits and munched on a handful of desiccated apricots and peaches, to restore his energy and to give him some quick strength for the final climb ahead. As he ate, he looked up from his crouched position to survey the steeple, where a flock of swallows circled the top, and was pleased to see that at close range the surface of it was just as it appeared in his photos: blocks of gray stone with deep crevices between each stone and rough, dimpled surfaces for excellent hand-grips.

Stuffing the dried fruit back in his pack, he checked to see that all was in readiness: the safety belt, the length of nylon rope, the condoms, and, most important of all, the bulkily folded up banner. As for the roofer's tool belt, having served its purpose, he unsnapped it from around his waist and dropped it in the rain gutter running around the steeple's base, making him that much lighter for the arduous climb—and, afterwards, his possible escape. Then, taking the nylon rope, he made a lariat of it and, having been practicing for days on a high tree branch in Tompkins Square, aimed at a gargoyle high up on the steeple—the very same gargoyle he'd noted in his photos—and twirling the rope slung it up into the air. Damn, if one of the swallows, he was amazed to see, didn't dart from the flock, nip the noose in its beak and flip it over the gargoyle's head, lassoing its scrawny neck expertly. "A good omen," Tom grinned and, tugging the rope hard to make sure it was snug, he took the ends in his hands and tied them in a slipknot around his waist, at that moment not only thanking the swallow but thanking his father for forcing him into the Boy Scouts at an early age.

Now all he had to do was squat down and be patient.

The noise of the gathering crowd, the chanting, had now grown into a roar. Lifting himself a little out of his crouch, he peeped around the base of the steeple and leaned out over the low stone balustrade of the facade only as much as he dared, so as not to be spotted, in order to view the scene below.

What he saw out on 5th Avenue amazed him. He'd been to demos with big crowds before, but he was surprised to see, even before the time set for this one to begin, thousands and thousands of activists and protesters milling in the streets below, waving a sea of placards and banners, and mixing with the rather worried-looking churchgoers scurrying up the broad, main steps of The Cathedral. There were also growing hordes of police on foot and on horseback, many in riot gear, making it look like an armed encampment.

There was a wall of STOP signs: STOP CHURCH INTERFERENCE IN OUR LIVES! There were scores of posters with the profile photo of The Cardinal, reading STOP THE CHURCH and STOP THIS MAN, as well as others that proclaimed THE CARDINAL WANTS TO JOIN OPERATION RESCUE: KEEP OUR ABORTION CLINICS OPEN—STOP THIS MAN, and PUBLIC ENEMY AND PUBLIC HEALTH MENACE, with a sinister, grainy photo of The Cardinal wearing goofy glasses with dizzy spirals on the lenses. There were others that read CURB YOUR DOGMA and DANGER: NARROWMINDED CHURCH AHEAD, and a poster so huge a man and a woman had to carry it:

THE 7 DEADLY SINS OF THE CARDINAL:
ASSAULT ON LESBIANS AND GAYS

BIAS
IGNORANT DENIAL
ENDANGERING WOMEN'S LIVES
NO SAFE SEX EDUCATION
NO CONDOMS
NO CLEAN NEEDLES

There were even signs in Yiddish carried by members of a gay and lesbian synagogue: FLY *FEYGELE!* and *FREYLEKH* FOLK ARE THE BEST FOLKS! and MAYBE ALL THE CARDINAL NEEDS IS A *KEPY*—IT WOULDN'T HOIT! And the grim SHVAYGEN = TOYT (Silence = Death).

There were signs in Spanish: ACTIVISTAS UNIDOS CONTRA EL SIDA and EL CARDINAL TIENE SANGRE EN SUS MANOS! (The Cardinal has blood on his hands!).

There were signs waved in support, and to the beat of a drum, by the Native American gay and lesbian group, We Wah & Bar-Chee-Ampee.

There were signs carried by FAP (Females Against Phallocracy) and SNIP (Sisters Network Invalidating Patriarchy) as well as signs carried by women from WHEN and WHAM!, the groups Deirdre and Kitty belonged to (groups whose spelled out names and aims had given His Eminence conniptions in his toilet earlier):

SISTER, DON'T FORGET THE DAM
(DIKES SAVE CITIES)

And:

SISTERS ARE DOIN' IT FOR THEMSELVES
WE'RE TAKING ABORTION INTO OUR OWN
HANDS!

130

and

> WE DON'T NEED MEN TO HAVE SEX!
> WE DON'T WANT TO HAVE TO
> *CASTRATE* ANYONE
> (We Know Who You Are)

Behind "The 7 Deadly Sins" sign, one protester carried a triptych of photos: Mussolini on the left, Hitler on the right, and in the middle, The Cardinal himself, flashing one of his most photogenic smiles, and under the photos, one bold black word: BROTHERS.

And finally there was one enormous banner that read simply:

> *ALL* PEOPLE WITH AIDS ARE INNOCENT

Yes, thought Tom, from his lofty perch, eyeing the signs and banners and the growing crowds swarming below, it was a vast success already.

His vision shifted across 5th Avenue, where Rockefeller Center loomed, its long line of garden pools with their bronze carp fountains rimmed brilliantly with familiar and exotic spring flowers, with tourists and strollers by the hundreds already crowding its walks and resting on its stone benches, many with heads turned curiously and apprehensively to the baffling uproar out on 5th Avenue around The Cathedral, and on a Sunday morning, too.

Tom The Trickster also noted that a number of mini-cam TV vans were parked on the side streets of Rockefeller Center—ABC, CBS, NBC, and all the local channels—who, along with the police, were evidently also alerted well in advance, undoubtedly long before ACT UP's and the other groups' press releases. The satellite aerials on the roofs of their trucks shot up like telephone poles almost as high as to where Tom himself was perched behind the steeple, with his panoramic view of all the hubbub that was going on in the streets below him.

He shifted his eyes from the scene to the lofty steeple rearing itself high in the sky, and where the flock of swallows still circled. Soon he would be mounting it; he felt a tremendous rush of excitement, as if he were about to have great sex.

He couldn't stop grinning to himself and reached into his backpack for another fistful of mixed fruits, washing them down with a swig of Asmaralda's brew that he brought along with him in its mayonnaise jar.

Asmaralda was also there, of course, now circling the steeple in the form of one of those swallows, keeping an eye on Tom The Trickster and his lasso tricks, keeping an eye on The Demo, and on all the activists and demonstrators below, particularly keeping an eye out for Peter The Poet, whom she'd last left at the site of the old Everard Baths on West 28th and who was now slipping nervously past a cordon of cops as he crossed East 50th Street; and keeping an eye out for Deirdre The Rad Dyke and her Kitty, who, having made their way up out of the subway station, were now also nearing The Cathedral, but on the East 51st Street side.

Like the other swallows flying around the steeple of the church, where they persisted in making their home no matter how often, because of the bird lime, The Cardinal tried, through the services of The Blue Bird Ornithologic Exterminating Company, to drive them out (he'd had more success driving out those other "queer birds" in Dignity who were, to His Eminence, also like bird-doo on the face of The Church), Tom and Asmaralda had the best bird's eye view of all that was happening in the streets below.

And also at that very instant, at the north corner of East 50th Street, Peter The Poet encountered the same beggar who, having been thrown off the Number 6 train by the transit police for the third time that morning, had earlier rattled his soiled paper cup at Tom The Trickster on the uptown train, as he did later at Skint The Skinhead; but Peter was, as Tom had been, so intent on his caper and, as said, on the men and women in blue, who were everywhere it seemed, he ignored the outthrust cup and rushed by the beggar without seeing him, as he pushed his way to the front of the barricades.

Meanwhile, back inside the sacristy, which like every interior within The Cathedral, not to mention The Chancellory itself, was the color of Mrs. Rafferty's meatloaf (overdone, just as His Excellency liked it), The Cardinal himself, with the assistance of his faithful servant, Brother Francis, was suiting up for high mass. Behind them, standing quietly, reverently, one might say, against a dark-paneled wall engraven with the heads of saints and angels, stood the aforementioned array of church and political dignitaries, for, as it had been considered an especial favor in the Court of King Louis XIV, The Sun King, to be invited to watch His Majesty at his *levée,* that is, performing his morning ablutions, even to his squatting on the royal commode—behind a discreet silk tapestry screen, of course (it was a signal honor, naturally, to be chosen to wipe the Royal *Derrière*)—and to observe the royal robing of The Monarch by his courtiers, so it was also considered an honor to be invited to the sacristy of The Cathedral of a Sunday morning to observe His Excellency prepare for mass, a ritual instigated by The Cardinal himself because he knew how much pleasure it would give those whom God, speaking through The Pope, of course, had not elevated to such a blessed position as himself.

Even The Mayor, although he was a Jew, was there, but many, including Monsignor Malinowski, did not think this odd, saying His Honor seemed more Catholic sometimes than The Cardinal himself.

Brother Francis actually oversaw the more humble tasks, such as making sure there was not a scuff, nay, not even so much as a speck of dust, on The Cardinal's already highly polished black oxfords—The Cardinal was most particular about that. He had also to check for any loose threads or wrinkles in any of the fabrics of the numerous ceremonial garments His Grace put on—more rich and costly garments, said the tart-tongued Monsignor, than King Louis Himself ever wore— or, heaven forbid, as happened not too many Sundays ago! when a raveling gold thread was discovered by the good Brother in the hem of The Cardinal's royal purple satin cope with the embroidered gold around the shoulders, then Brother Francis had had to play emergency seamstress, plying the needle he always kept in a sewing kit in the coarse folds of his own hopsack robe, since no females, naturally, not even Mrs. Rafferty, were permitted in the *sanctum sanctorum* of the sacristy during the vesting of His Eminence.

134

Then, too, it was a sign of special favor to be permitted by The Cardinal, a privilege Monsignor Malinowski, it goes without saying, had never been granted, to help him on, as The Cardinal muttered the appropriate prayer for each vestment, with the more elaborate raiment: his chasuble, his aforementioned cope, or finally to place on his head, like a tall crown, his peaked miter—while Brother Francis whispered an aside to the lucky "crowner" to be careful not to muss a hair of The Cardinal's carefully oiled pompadour—the very same miter His Eminence was wearing in the notorious ACT UP "KNOW YOUR SCUMBAG" poster photo, right alongside of which was the photo of the unrolled, oversized, bright-pink condom, the very same poster that numerous activists outside The Cathedral were at that very moment waving about on long poles.

Through the tall, slender stained-glass windows of the sacristy, letting in their slanting, rainbow-speckled mid-morning light, The Cardinal could hear the increasing roar of these protesters out in front of his Cathedral.

> "ACT UP! WE'RE HERE!
> WE'RE LOUD AND RUDE,
> PRO-CHOICE AND QUEER!"

came clearly through the narrow leaded windows.

"The usual riffraff," murmured Brother Francis, all innocence, as he spit on a scabrous finger and rubbed it into the toe of The Cardinal's left shoe, to bring up the shine.

The Cardinal smiled inwardly. He, of course, knew, right down to the last detail, all that would go on that morning during The Demonstration. Plain clothes detectives and plain cops in civvies, particularly those from predominantly Irish and Italian parishes throughout the city, and most loyal to His Eminence, had eagerly volunteered for Operation Disordered; so many, in fact, had offered their services that precinct captains had had to turn a number away. Now, packing their gats in shoulder harnesses beneath their Sunday suit jackets—it was from just such a harness Peter The Poet, who was at that very moment elbowing his way toward the front of the barricades, had slipped the semi-automatic from the tipsy off-duty detective on the West Street piers, a semi-automatic that was now riding on the back of The Poet concealed in his knapsack—these "security men," and women, were at that very moment scattered throughout the pews in readiness, waiting, along with hundreds of others of the more militant loyal parishioners, whom The Cardinal's "God's eyes" had tipped off in advance, for The Cardinal's high mass to begin.

So The Cardinal knew all of these carefully planned details, for his dear friend, The Mayor, had whispered them in his ear just moments before in the sacristy, knew all of them except, of course, for the fact that two individuals who squatted in the same abandoned tenement of The Mayor's down on Avenue D had separate plans for him: one to sock him in the jaw; the other to blow his brains out; both of whom were now adding their voices to the chants and cries of the growing hordes in the streets outside the sacristy windows.

These details, however, neither The Mayor's secret police nor The Cardinal's own "God's eyes" had been able to uncover.

"We must be charitable, my dear Brother Francis," oozed The Cardinal, for a bare instant the fiery stakes of The Inquisition blazing in his mind's eye, an involuntary sigh escaping his lips as he thought of The Good Old Days.

Torquemada would've known how to handle this mob of heretics.

He glanced surreptitiously down at his shoe tops peeping out the hems of his robes, just to make sure no flakes of Brother Francis's psoriasis marred their gleaming surface.

Now Brother Francis was carefully combing down The Cardinal's mustache, making sure, since he knew how sensitive The Cardinal was about it, that it covered every trace of his hare lip.

One last bit of business to be done: Brother Francis now whipped from the folds of his robe an atomizer filled with Holy Water (blessed by The Pope's own hand) and a bit of chamois and, spraying The Cardinal's glasses with a few dainty squeezes of the atomizer's bulb, polished the lenses clean, since The Cardinal could not abide spotty eye glasses anymore than he could abide spotty Waterford crystal goblets on his dinner table, as Mrs. Rafferty well knew, having caught the rough edge of his tongue once or twice. And, since the Holy Water had been blessed especially by The Pope, The Cardinal believed it helped him to see God's Will more clearly.

When Brother Francis had given the last wipe, His Eminence turned and lifting his arms in a Christ-like gesture, attempting to imitate Him in spirit if not in dress, gave the onlookers against the wall his blessing—giving a quick, special wink at The Mayor himself: The Cardinal thought it was so cute, having a Jew in his sacristy, and such a dear Jew.

The Mayor, whose once-flaming red hair still flamed—with the help, some said, of L'Oréal— blushed as red as his unruly thatch.

Through the kindness of His Excellency, he

would be saying a few words after The Cardinal's homily, as if it were just another of those political events so dear to his, and to The Cardinal's, heart.

"I am ready," pronounced The Cardinal, and those who were especially selected to escort him to the altar and to serve mass for him on this particular Sunday, fell into procession at the sacristy door, including his bodyguard of three retired cops in their high-mass clerical drag, one of them, as noted, a black belt in karate.

After The Cardinal and his entourage had headed out through the long passageway leading to the massive altar of The Cathedral, Brother Francis slipped out a side door of the sacristy and, scurrying through a maze of narrow, winding corridors and up dark spiral staircases, made his way through the labyrinthine back passages of The Cathedral into a short hallway that connected with The Chancellory. Climbing a series of well-worn, rickety servants stairs, he hurriedly made his way up to the attic and his cell of a room, eager to get a glimpse of all the activity surrounding The Cathedral and its environs that unusual Sunday morning. Once there, he raced to the single tiny slot of a window under the eaves and looked down. Even from that height and with the window shut, he could clearly hear the chants and shouts of the angry activists massed in the streets below. As he listened, a benevolent smile creased the plump cheeks of his angelic face as he rubbed his hands excitedly.

Flinging open the window to get a better view, out of the corner of his eye he caught a flicker of movement out beyond the steep, tiled roofs of The Cathedral, and looking saw the most amazing sight: someone, with a belt of worker's tools and a bulging backpack scattered at his feet, was, with apparently the aid of one of the swallows The Cardinal detested, attempting to lasso a rope around the neck of one of the gargoyles on the steeple, someone, as Brother Francis caught a glimpse of his face in profile, he was quite familiar with from ACT UP interviews on the television news, someone in fact who, not only by his face and figure but by his words as well, had inspired the good Brother to make those secret pre-dawn telephone calls.

He rubbed his hands even more excitedly, the psoriasis spots on their backs glowing redder and redder as he rubbed.

By the time Peter The Poet crossed 50th Street and merged with the crowd in front of The Cathedral, and Deirdre The Rad Dyke and her Kitty rounded the corner at 51st Street to do the same, the crowds had grown to well over 6,000. The police, of course, as they appeared to do for any march or demonstration they considered "dangerous" or threatening to the status quo, would, to diminish its effect, tell The Media there were only "about 1,000" at The Demo; the only accurate figures for crowds they ever seemed to give the press were for the Saint Patrick's Day Parade, the Columbus Day Parade, their own protest actions (when, for instance, civilians wanted *real* civilians on The Civilian Review Board), or any parade in which The Patrolmen's Benevolent Association marched.

Speaking of Saint Patrick and Columbus, Peter The Poet wondered was it his imagination or did an inordinate number of the cops' faces look Irish and Italian? (Perhaps Irish and Italian *Catholic?*) Had there been a directive to that effect, he continued to wonder, whispered by The Cardinal in The Mayor's shell-like ear while they sipped their sherry in front of the fire in The Cardinal's Chancellory bedroom, after which His Honor, who was rumored, among the more tart-tongued, to be "queer for cops," whispered it to The Police Commissioner who in turn sent word out to all the precinct captains in the city who in turn dispatched these hordes of Cardinal-sympathetic cops, truncheons in hand, to keep "order"?

How queer also, Peter thought, that The Mayor's limo was parked out front on this particular occasion, to attend his pal The Cardinal's mass. But was it really that unusual? Some, including The Poet, thought of The Chancellory as "the other City Hall."

The butterflies began to swarm again in Peter's belly, since everywhere he looked were cops; he shuddered to think how many others were here in plain-clothes.

Nervously, he once again patted his knapsack, where the semi-automatic was hidden.

And there was that subway beggar again! now being hustled off the steps of The Cathedral by a male and female cop team because he was undoubtedly seen as unfit to enter "God's Holy Place," as The Cardinal loved to phrase it.

And there stood, as they had been standing year after year since The Lesbian-Gay Pride March started marching down 5th Avenue past The Cathedral, the hardy band of "religious loonies," as Peter called them, squeezed in behind the police barriers across the Avenue at the corner of West 51st Street. Wearing their military-style berets and outfits, several of them were sprinkling the "wicked" activists with Holy Water, while others, endlessly chanting their Hail Marys, held up their rosary beads as a kind of shield against the "evil" mob in front of The Cathedral, or held aloft their own placards, all of them printed in large, bold white letters on black backgrounds: GOD HAD BURNT UP SODOM AND GOMORAH (Sic) and ABORTION IS THE WORK OF SATAN and PERVERTS ON PARADE OR SODOMITES ON FILTH and THE LORD WILL TAKE THIS *SICK-NESS* AWAY FROM YOU and REPENT SODOM-ITES! REPENT BABY MURDERERS!

These were the followers of Veronica Leuken, who alleged she often had visions of Jesus Christ and the Virgin Mary at the old World's Fair grounds in Flushing Meadows, near Rikers Is-land prison, and where this same Leuken Brigade said the rosary on a regular basis, avidly praying for more visions and for the end of sodomy and abortion.

A group of nearby men and women bearing a banner reading QUEER NATION began chants of "YOU SAY, 'DON'T FUCK!' WE SAY, 'FUCK YOU!' " their shouting, including Deirdre's and Kitty's, who joined them, rising above the Hail Marys, as several of Leuken's devotees, with increased ar-dor, continued to sprinkle the chanters with Holy Water, as if trying to put out a raging fire beyond their control.

Through the vast open bronze doors of The Ca-thedral, with their figures of saints embossed on their surface, came the thundrous opening notes of the huge pipe organ followed by the swelling voice of the choir up in its loft, harmonious voices, in contrast to the cries of the street, lifting themselves in a hymn of praise to God The Father.

The light in the open doorway of The Cathedral was the color of dark honey, "and twice as seduc-tive," thought The Poet, bitterly.

And also slipping up the broad steps among the regular mass-goers was a number of young men whom Peter, now pressed against the barricades so that he could not move, recognized as familiar faces from ACT UP meetings, all dressed up, like the undercover cops already inside, in their Sunday best suits and ties, but concealing in the pockets of *their* suit jackets not guns but coiled lengths of heavy-duty chains, the chains wrapped in Kleenex so as not to rattle as they walked.

Once inside, the young men scattered throughout the pews, finding seats wherever they could of the few that remained, several sitting together in twos and threes, but most of them sitting alone. Once seated, each assumed a quiet, attentive expression.

Meanwhile, out in the middle of 5th Avenue, the crowd had respectfully cleared a space for a number of People With AIDS to conduct a die-in, dozens of them lying down corpse-like in the street while others, with cans of spray paint, outlined their bodies in white against the pitch-black of the asphalt; then, when "the dead" had arisen, they stenciled within the ghostly outline: ONE PERSON WITH AIDS DIES EVERY HOUR.

And when they had finished, a group of women lay down in the street, and other women with cans of red paint outlined the bodies of those women, and when they rose up, the former also stenciled words within the outlined bodies: A WOMAN HAS JUST DIED BECAUSE OF A BACK ALLEY ABORTION—KEEP ABORTION LEGAL KEEP ABORTION SAFE.

The hush that followed the stenciling of the bodies in the center of the Avenue was replaced with a low and angry hum that grew into a steady roar of chants and cries, a cacaphony of all the disparate—and desperate—voices howling out in front of The Cathedral:

"STOP THE CHURCH!"
"CURB ITS DOGMAS!"
"CONDOMS NOW!"
"CLEAN NEEDLES NOW!"
"SEX EDUCATION NOW!"

A woman raised a sign high above the others: ARREST MOTHER TERESA FOR CRIMES AGAINST WOMEN! while another woman shouted over the Avenue at the praying Leukenites: "KEEP YOUR ROSARIES OFF MY OVARIES!"

One of the women of Queer Nation thrust into Deirdre's hands an extra placard on a pole, from the batch she was passing out, which turned out to be one of the STOP THE CHURCH placards with its photo of The Cardinal in profile, à la Hollywood, which Peter The Poet had noted plastered everywhere in his hike up Broadway. Deirdre swung it aloft, waving it vigorously in the faces of the police in riot gear guarding the wooden barriers the crowds were penned behind, and at the last of the parishioners scurrying up the steps and into The Cathedral, Deirdre now pleased to have a message on a stick to wave along with her Kitty whose placard, with its clit-pink message of STOP VIOLENCE/AGAINST LESBIANS, was barely visible over the heads of those engulfing her diminutive body, both women shouting in unison with the others in Queer Nation: "STOP THE CHURCH! TAX THE CHURCH! STOP THE CHURCH! TAX THE CHURCH!"

Meanwhile, Skint The Skinhead, clutching Corkie behind a nearby police barrier, was busily scanning the crowd for "dat poivoit from THROW UP," as he snidely called it, whom he'd seen several times in TV interviews, unaware that Tom The Trickster was concealed at that very moment up behind the steeple on The Cathedral's roof, awaiting his moment and looking down on all the crowd, including, with his easily recognizable polished skull, Skint The Skinhead, who he realized was the one whom he'd had to outrun any number of times in the streets of Alphabet City. Tom wished, at the very least, he had water to fill one of the condoms in his backpack to drop at that very moment on that head that was, to him, "as empty of hair as it was apparently of everything else."

Skint then shoved his way in at the other end of the barricade, snatching Corkie along behind, and instead of spotting Tom spotted Deirdre and Kitty, instantly recognizing them as "da' pair a' dyke love boids" on the subway. What caught his eye even more was the photo on the poster Deirdre was swinging wildly about. Although Skint was no friend of The Church—since his final days at La Salle Academy he'd come to loathe all authoritative institutions, except for The Third Reich, "in Da' Good Ole Days," as he called them—The Cardinal, as has been intimated, was "a real right-stuff hero" of his, along with, of course, Adolf Hitler, ex-President Reagan, and "the Duke," as Skint affectionately referred to David Duke, the recently-elected legislator in Louisiana, former grand wizard of the Knights of the Klu Klux Klan in that region, and founder of The National Association for the Advancement of White People.

Using his massive arms and shoulders and snaking his hips to advantage, he bulled his way through the crowd pressing up against the barrier, ripped the sign out of Deirdre's hands, ducked under the barricade and, snatching Corkie by the hair, was off and away, racing toward

144

West 52nd Street before Deirdre or Kitty or anyone else knew what had happened.

"*Arrest him! Arrest him!*" Deirdre and Kitty
and several other women around them shouted,
but the cops maintained their stone-faced, unseeing expressions, as if nothing had happened.

However, a couple of Pink Panthers, the lesbian
and gay male group that patroled the streets of
the East and West Village after dark, in basic gay-
guerrilla black, with the emblem of a black pan-
ther paw print inside a pink triangle decaled on
their black T-shirts, spotted what had happened
and chased after the retreating Skint, dressed in
his all-black outfit, and catching up with him before he reached West 52nd, struggled to wrestle
the sign from his grasp. But Skint, gripping the
sign pole tighter in his meaty fists, swiftly
smacked each of the Pink Panthers over the skull
with the butt end, stunning them, and again
snatching Corkie by the ends of her long hair,
tore off into the crowd and around the corner.

More cries of "*Arrest him! Arrest him!*" rose up
among those nearby who had seen the bashing,
their fingers pointing at the swiftly disappearing
leather-jacketed back of Skint; but instead of
chasing after him, several of the stony-faced cops
hurdled the barrier and, wading in with truncheons raised, yanked the dazed Pink Panthers
up from the asphalt, kneed them in the back,
cuffed them, and marched them off double-step to
the police vans parked on either side of East 51st
Street, while the crowd shouted, "SHAME!
SHAME! SHAME!"

Meanwhile, Skint The Skinhead, ducking into
a doorway on West 52nd, whipped out his spray
paint can and, after crossing out its STOP THE
CHURCH proclamation, aerosoled in big letters in

the space above His Eminence's carefully-lighted photo: KILL A KOCKSUCKER FOR THE KARDNAL! (sic). Then, dragging Corkie along behind him, he sauntered nonchalantly to the corner where he and Corkie mingled among the band of Veronica Leuken devotees, in their military berets and garb, who were still holding their rosary beads aloft and chanting their Hail Marys at the activists, while Skint, blending easily among them in *his* stormtrooper-type outfit, grinning victoriously from ear to ear, held up his own version of Deirdre's and ACT UP's placard, amid the boldly lettered white on black placards of the Leukenites, all of whom were so busy praying and sprinkling the "wicked" with Holy Water and holding their own biblical messages on high, they failed to read the message in bright red that had just come among them.

Meanwhile, Brother Francis was trotting back down the winding stairs from his attic room to the main body of The Cathedral, where he stood in the shadowy wings off the main altar, waiting to hear The Cardinal's homily, standing not far, in fact, from the very spot where Monsignor Malinowski was alleged to have spied the cardinal nicknamed "Fanny" on his knees, "at prayer." The very much alive current Cardinal, however, in his splendid purple and gold raiment, was just at that moment lifting The Host high before the gold door of the tabernacle, his angular face emblazoned in massed candlelight.

Brother Francis stood quietly in the shadow, except that now and then his hands stirred agitatedly beneath the folds of his hopsack robe, that cherubic grin still creasing his own flushed face.

146

High up above the heads of his parishioners in his stone pulpit on the altar of The Cathedral, before reading from his prepared text, The Cardinal gestured toward the front doors and intoned into the microphone on the lectern: "My dear brethren. Outside the doors of this holy place, we hear a great perturbation. We hear the misguided cries of The Disturbed and The Disordered, who have all our compassion. But, I must speak The Truth, which is, of course, God's Truth, and I say those who practice homosexual acts and those who practice abortion are, I repeat, in God's Name, in God's Truth, The Disordered and The Disturbed, for they are all murderers in their own way, in God's eyes."

Then, through the gleamingly polished lenses of his glasses, dropping his own eyes to his prepared text, he began reading his homily thusly: "We, as good, as devout, Catholics believe the truths of God, and one of those eternal truths is the sanctity of marriage, that the great gift of sexuality given to us by God be used to serve Him by procreation within the bounds of holy matrimony . . ."

Now, hearing his voice reecho back to him, that mellifluous voice amplified a hundredfold and reverberating through the huge loudspeakers of the state-of-the-art Dolby Sound System, especially installed by The Cardinal himself—"Making his voice more resonant than God's," commented Monsignor Malinowski acidly, as might be expected—loudspeakers placed high up at intervals along The Cathedral walls, including, since his homilies were so popular, outside ones hung on either side of the great front doors for

147

the overflow crowd in the streets to hear his every word—his every word on this particular Sunday morning more often than not drowned out by the chants of the thousands of protesters packed in front of The Cathedral. Now hearing his words resonate in his own ears, The Cardinal envisioned them as engendering countless infants for the love of God and he . . . *he* . . . their spiritual father! For the moment, he seemed to sway at the lectern and grasped the edge of the pulpit, just as he'd clutched the edge of the ancient sink in The Chancellory toilet earlier that morning, his eyes once again rolling up in a swoon as he conceived himself once more not only as "the father of thousands" now, but of millions . . .

The Dolby Sound System certainly did have that effect on him.

Recovering himself, he continued, "But we have here today, as I have already mentioned, dearly beloved, outside this holy House of God, a great confusion, a disturbance by those who are disturbed in their minds about The Church's position on doctrinal matters of birth control and homosexuality, those who would have us change the teachings of The Church to please them. But this we cannot do, because, as you well know, the teachings of The Church are The Truth of God and that Truth we cannot and will not change . . . *ever . . .*"

Outside, at these words blasting through the loudspeakers, the roar, of boos, mainly, grew louder.

The Cardinal paused momentarily, baffled by the sight of several young men rising from their pews, stepping into the aisles, and calmly, deliberately, lying down on their backs, closing their eyes and clasping their hands over their chests, as if they were lying asleep—or, as The Cardinal quickly imagined (quickly wished, too, for he had not been told there would be trouble *inside* The Cathedral), they were lying dead in their coffins.

"Our own security and The Mayor's secret police . . . er, plainclothes men . . . will soon take care of the matter," he thought complacently, for all possible contingencies had been anticipated between his and The Mayor's staffs; and in the same soothing, measured tones, with the voice of calm, sweet reason, he continued his homily.

"The Church has compassion for those who suffer, particularly for those who suffer from AIDS. Have not I, at the opening of our very own Mother Teresa Hospice" (at mention of her name through the loudspeakers outside, there were loud hisses from the crowds in the street), "have I not emptied and washed the bedpans of those poor benighted victims?" he continued, his voice ringing fervently to the very heights of the vaulted ceiling—and hadn't he said this, unashamedly, right in front of the TV cameras at the ribbon-cutting ceremonies officially opening the hospice the day after? Not mentioning, of course, his profoundly held belief, that was also God's and, hence, also The Pope's, so, naturally, it was his, that many in that hospice wouldn't have the disease if they hadn't lived out their own "homosexual disease"; conveniently not mentioning either, that it was Brother Francis who'd actually been stuck with the unpleasant bedpan-cleaning duty. But that was neither here nor there in The Cardinal's eyes: his *spirit* had been willing—and, after all, he was such a busy man of God . . . *and* Brother Francis did so love to serve—look how well he served His Eminence—and with his psoriasis, was not the good Brother himself also afflicted in his own way and hence the more readily compassionate? And by performing such humble tasks was he not making points in Heaven? And was it not un-Christian to stand in the way of another's salvation? etc., etc.

The Cardinal, too, agreed with that fool Cardinal in Puerto Rico who had had the idiocy to say, right out loud in front of The Media, if you please, "It is better they die of AIDS than that they use condoms"; that was to be expected of the passionate Latin temperament, but The Cardinal himself, of course, would *never, never* speak such beliefs aloud, no matter how fervently he held them, since they might be misconstrued as "unChrist-like."

Always remember what the eyes of the TV cameras see—and hear—was his watchword. Political, and American, to his fingertips, he knew, to repeat another of his watchwords, Image is all.

And that was why, knowing good PR would offset what was going on outside in the streets, he had allowed the TV cameras, with their bright lights, inside The Cathedral, during his homily.

Aloud now he himself said into the mike, "However, my dear brethren, good morality is good medicine."

And he liked that phrase so much, one of his "inspirations" while "sitting on the throne" a few mornings earlier, that he said it again.

Hearing it repeated, the furious roar of the swarms in the streets shot up several decibels.

As more and more young men, joined now by women, stepped out of their pews and lay down in the aisles, a voice was heard shouting above the Dolby-generated echoes of The Cardinal's last words. Startled, The Cardinal peered out over the heads of his flock and . . . well, not surprised exactly, since it had happened before (with that Dignity rabble standing up in silent protest with their backs turned during his homilies! He'd had to get a court injunction against that lot) but, rather, he was taken aback to see a very pale, very thin—one might have described him as "AIDS-thin"—young man clutching the back of the pew in front of him for support as he spoke in a voice surprisingly strong for one so feeble-looking: "You preach love but you practice hate!"

Others now throughout the vast congregation began to rise from their seats and speak out, "affinity groups who had secretly planned civil disobedience," as was later reported. Some arose to pray aloud, but mostly, all over The Cathedral, discordant voices were heard, echoing like The Cardinal's had, up to the very roof of the Cathedral, upon which Tom The Trickster still crouched, banner furled and ready, waiting his main chance.

"We of The Church are compassionate . . ." breathed The Cardinal, leaning into the mike.

"The people of The Church may be but the hierarchy is not!" loudly interrupted a protester.

Shouts were now heard throughout The Cathedral.

"Stop Church interference in our lives!"

"The Cardinal is a fake Christian! Throw him out of this holy place!"

Undoubtedly one of "that lot" from Dignity, thought The Cardinal, heatedly. His hare lip beneath its mustache quivered noticeably, but he quickly recovered. The shouters were all obviously some poor AIDS-demented creatures and not to be taken seriously.

One undoubtedly literary type shouted from the rear, "The Cardinal is the murderer in The Cathedral!"

"He murders women's lives!" yelled a woman, leaping up from a pew near the front.

"He murders gays, he murders lesbians, with

151

his hate!" croaked an elderly man on the far side of the nave.

Hearing that, as if on cue, a number of men and women kept popping up from their pews and shouting, "Murderer! Murderer!" then quickly sitting down again, only to pop up again and shout, "Murderer!"

Amidst the cries, there was the distinct rattling of chains.

The Cardinal turned ashen. For perhaps one of the few times in his life he was struck speechless. And also for the first time, as they zeroed in on the scene and also caught close-up reactions of The Cardinal's own face, he definitely wished he'd not permitted TV cameras inside The Cathedral.

However, he soon regained his composure and droned on, citing the old chestnut, "We love the sinner but hate the sin," then quoted another Cardinal's pastoral letter, intoning, "No one should be surprised when a 'morally offensive lifestyle is physically attacked.'"

Skint The Skinhead, hearing this blast through the loudspeakers outside The Cathedral, put a small finger in either corner of his mouth and whistled shrilly. Peter The Poet, his own fingers for the umpteenth time reassuringly caressing the steely imprint of the semi-automatic through the nylon of his knapsack, heard the gravelly rumble of The Cardinal's honeyed tones through those same outdoor speakers and felt a chill go through him, his Mind's Eye vividly picturing similar loudspeakers he'd seen on TV in old newsreels, fixed high up on lamp posts, also blaring voices in the streets of Berlin in the 1930s.

Hearing those words of The Cardinal, another angry roar arose from the crowds seething in front of The Cathedral. The Cardinal was just about to utter, "Naturally, being people of God, being compassionate, we don't want to see anyone harmed . . ." when suddenly his voice, droning through the outside speakers, diminished, as one by one the highly sophisticated stereo speakers went dead, thanks to Asmaralda flying down from the church steeple and with her tiny but powerful swallow's beak (given a shot of extra bite by Big Sister), unplugging one at a time the Dolby speakers hanging on the outside walls of The Cathedral.

The crowd roared its approval at this sudden "failure" of electric power.

Back inside, the clinking rattle of chains increased as a number of people began chaining themselves to their pews. The hard metallic snapping of padlocks was heard throughout the vast space.

Several more began to handcuff themselves to the armrests of the benches.

More and more people stepped out of the pews to lie down in the aisles.

Now the eyes of the vast majority of the congregation were no longer on The Cardinal—an observation that caused His Eminence a noticeable moment of pique—those "disturbed and disordered" creatures were stealing his show! Most of the congregation were becoming uneasy, an increasing number were becoming downright alarmed, especially when one man—who was later said to be an ex-altar boy (and a member of Dignity)—walked calmly down the aisle and deliberately hurled on the stone floor in front of the elevated pulpit where The Cardinal stood, the consecrated Communion wafer he'd earlier palmed during the communion service.

"If what you speak is God's compassion, then you can have it!" shouted the youth. "I think Jesus would be ashamed of you!"

A gasp went up from the flock. The Cardinal, his lower lip quivering now, clutched the edge of the lectern much as the AIDS-thin youth who had first spoken out had gripped the back of the pew for support.

The ex-altar boy was shouting something about "heartlessness" and "inhumanity" and also calling The Cardinal a "murderer," as he was being hauled off by Cathedral security to a side exit and thrust into the arms—and billy clubs—of the waiting police.

Some activists now were tossing among the devout what looked suspiciously to The Cardinal to be packets of rainbow-tinted condoms.

His Eminence immediately signaled to the choir loft for organ music.

Still visibly shaken, he also signaled his dear friend The Mayor, who simply stood and nodded his thatch of red hair briefly in a certain direction, for the plainclothes police, heavily scattered among the pews and along the rear walls of The Cathedral, to remove the protesters. Which they did, moving swiftly and silently to carry off the limp bodies lying in the "die-in" all up and down the aisles, and moving in with chain bolt cutters to quickly cut the shackles of those who had chained and handcuffed themselves to the pews, and hustled all of them out the side doors to the waiting police vans and buses on East 51st, where they were given the choke hold while being put into plastic handcuffs.

Surging down that side street, deliberately chosen by The Tactical Squad since it was out of sight of the main action in front of The Cathedral, hence away from the eyes of The Media, were a number of ACT UP members who, more hip to police methods and, so, running ahead of the TV camera people, surrounded the police who, in their yellow industrial-strength rubber gloves to avoid phantom contagion from those whom they had hauled out of The Cathedral, were slinging those same protesters into the rear of the vans like so many sides of beef, the activists screaming, "SHAME! SHAME! SHAME!" over and over.

Some who arrived at the scene later, because they could not run and who joined in at the fringes of the crowd of shouters, were so ill with AIDS they could barely stand up, their throats so raspy with the fungus of thrush, they could barely be heard, but they also joined their voices to the chorus of protests.

Still, this didn't prevent the police from wading in among them, first slapping strips of black electrical tape over the names and numbers on their badges, their upraised truncheons democratically flailing left and right, batting down the strong and healthy along with those who were AIDS-wasted or spotted with the purple lesions of Kaposi's Sarcoma or ravaged with other infections.

"Fuckin' cacksuckuhs," muttered one of New York's Finest, as he smashed his club in the face of the youth who had first stood up to speak in The Cathedral and who dropped like a stone and began to cough blood on the asphalt. A few drops spattered on the highly polished black Official New York Patrolman's shoes of the officer, a shine as high as the one on The Cardinal's own brogans.

"Sonuvabitch!"

He swung his billy club high and brought it down once more, this time on the skull of the offending youth, who quivered hunched in the gutter, making gulping noises deep in his throat.

"See where yer buttfuckin' gotcha'?" he growled, echoing, in cruder language, of course, the more polishedly stated beliefs of his beloved

Cardinal, annoyed, in spite of all the overtime he was being paid by The Mayor, that he was going to miss the opening kickoff of the Giants exhibition football game on TV that afternoon with his cop buddies.

One of the protesters, wearing a headband of a torn off strip of yellow plastic police tape used at all crime scenes, reading DO NOT CROSS, who ran to the aid of the fallen youth, was himself wrestled to the street by three other cops who instantly positioned themselves expertly as a team: one kneeling on the interloper's face, another on his legs, and a third in his groin, the latter grinding his kneecap into the nuts with especial avidity.

The young man screamed in agony.

The moment the television cameras arrived, of course, the worst of the violence ceased, and the cops tore off the black tape covering their badges, as they continued to choke hold, cuff, and haul the remaining arrested activists up into the vans.

At that very same instant, there was a great flurry of activity at the great bronze doors at the front of The Cathedral, and the TV camera crews, racing back around the corner, rushed up the steps, sensing The Cardinal, and no doubt The Mayor—the saying in The Media went, If The Cardinal shows up, can Hizzonor be far behind?—was about to make an appearance, since The Media knew, as well as Monsignor Malinowski did, how much His Eminence loved a camera.

And, yes, despite urgent whisperings from his bodyguards in their clerical drag that he was in imminent danger, as The Cardinal, *sans* miter, looking ashen and shaken but still able to flash that world-famous smile for the cameras, emerged through the massive bronze doors to stand at the top of The Cathedral steps, The

Mayor, no slouch, either, when it came to a camera lens, directly behind him, the TV camera people shoving around them for a good angle, this was the chain of events:

At the sight of The Cardinal, an unholy roar went up from the crowds, which began to shove against the barricades with such force the police, locking arms, had all they could do to hold them back. Then some of the crowd, unable to control themselves, burst through the police lines at several points and swarmed up The Cathedral steps. In the confusion, Deirdre, swept along with Kitty up the south corner of the steps, saw her chance and, her eyes slits as she focused them on The Cardinal's jaw, shot back her massive right arm, her beefy knuckles clenched ready in a huge fist to deliver the haymaker she'd learned in her boxing lessons at The Women's Martial Arts Center; while Peter The Poet, seeing *his* chance, his right hand concealed in his partially unzipped knapsack as he clutched the semi-automatic inside it and held the knapsack up before him, advanced up the steps from the north corner, his eye focused on the elegantly hand-stitched target of The Sacred Heart of Jesus woven on the robe of The Cardinal, directly beneath which beat The Cardinal's own heart; while Skint The Skinhead, still unable to spot Tom The Trickster, his eyes, however, having kept focused for some time from across the Avenue on Deirdre's broad behind in its orange muu-muu, speedily left the rosary-chanting Leukenites, dragged Corkie across 5th Avenue and shoving his way up the middle of the angry swarm pushing up the steps, slipped behind Deirdre, his spray can at the ready, his thumb eager to pounce on the spray button, Deirdre's backside—a far easier target than The Cardinal's jaw (or heart)—too tempting a target to pass up (it was a wall, a sidewalk, to him, prime for graffiti)—and he already knew what he'd spray paint, with his trademark bum spelling, on that massive, orange surface: GASS FAGS DIKES AND BABBY KILLERS! (he prayed the TV cameras would zero in on it); and Asmaralda, still a swallow, after unplugging all the outdoor loudspeakers, was darting and flying around their heads, then swirling up over the steeple, then swooping down over the steps below, as swallows will do, flying around her squatter neighbors, keeping a sharp bird's eye on everything, on their every movement.

Including Tom The Trickster's who, with only his two dark eyes visible peeping over the balustrade, was waiting for the exact right moment to play his trick. When he heard the commotion at The Cathedral doors directly below him, saw the TV camera people rushing for that spot and the crowd breaking through the barricades, including Deirdre from one end of the steps, with Kitty holding onto her arm for dear life, and Peter, one hand thrust into his unzipped knapsack, from the other end, and all come surging up the broad stone stairs in one vast body, he knew, having banked on his being unable to resist The Media despite the dangers, that The Cardinal had made his appearance, and Tom knew, too, that his own moment had come.

Checking the nylon safety rope he'd earlier looped around the gargoyle's outstretched neck, he snapped on his safety belt, thrust his arms through the shoulder straps of his backpack and, as agile as a monkey, began climbing hand over hand up the stones of the steeple until he reached the gargoyle almost at the pinnacle. Wrapping his legs around this narrowest part of the spire and letting himself fall back on the safety of the rope, while still grasping the steeple between his knees, he swung his backpack around against his chest and reaching in pulled out the window washer's safety belt which he slid behind his kidneys, then buckled around the steeple itself, snapping the sturdy buckle tight and thus holding himself in place. This now left his hands free and, again reaching into his pack, he carefully withdrew the bolt of 75 foot folded banner and tying the rope at its top around the steeple, just beneath the gargoyle, turned his body slightly forward and, hanging out in space on the belt and holding the banner in his outstretched arms high over his head, he peered for an instant down at the mass confusion far, far below, then let it drop.

The moment The Cardinal emerged, blinking in the bright sunlight and in the intense hand-held lights of the TV mini-cam crews, Peter The Poet, swept along with The Media in all the disorder, lunged, as he'd planned, at one of the cameras at the base of the steps, screaming, "The Cardinal is an enemy of the people! The Cardinal's America's worst murderer!"

"Get that faggot offa' me!" shouted the mini-cam man at one of his female assistants, as he struggled up the steps, camera on shoulder.

"Git outa' here, you creep!" she hollered. "Let The Cawdnal talk! You don't have nothin' to say!"

"Look out fer the poivoit," muttered one of The Cardinal's bodyguards, the one with the black belt, speaking into the micro-mike hidden inside his dog collar—all The Cardinal's guards were not only in clerical drag but also wired for close-range one-to-one radio contact.

The Cardinal, who as we have already learned, had a sixth sense in knowing where any camera lens was at any given instant, even though he sensed possible risk at that very moment, especially from that scrawny-faced creature near the bottom of the steps trying to shout into a camera, a face twisted with fury, a skinny wretch, who looked possibly Jewish and like he most certainly reeked of BO—Still, despite the menace, the lure of the cameras was all-powerful, and The Cardinal turned, as in a coy minuet, first to one beckoning camera eye then to another at the top of the steps, as a bouquet of microphones was thrust in his face. Clicking on his most seductive public smile and lowering his voice a honeyed octave, as he'd been taught in homiletics class at the seminary, and as was his wont, especially for his TV appearances, he intoned, "God bless you all, and thank you for coming. Welcome to God's House."

The TV and radio newscasters were all shouting questions at once: "Your Excellency, what is your view of what's going on inside and outside your church today?" and "Your Holiness, do you think that women who have abortions should be brought up on murder charges?" while the assistants to the TV camera crews, hired for their muscle (including not a few women), began shoving away those activists who tried to get to the mikes to give *their* perspectives on The Demo, and the reasons behind it. But, as always, viewed as riffraff, they were muscled out of the picture, because it was always The Media's policy that what The Cardinal and The Mayor had to say in such situations was far more "newsworthy."

And The Cardinal always sounded so sweetly reasonable; The Mayor, in his bright red bush of Harpo hair, so entertainingly convincing, always good for a laugh; so American in his shoot from the hip first, ask questions later.

"It is a sad, sad day in America," sighed The

Cardinal into the thicket of TV and radio mikes, "when an unruly mob invades the House of God and disrupts a religious service . . . an anti-Catholic mob . . . most UnAmerican . . ." mouthing, in a sudden fervor of democratic spirit, the very words that Tom The Trickster and others in ACT UP and WHAM! had predicted.

The Mayor, again, no slouch when it came to hogging a camera and who was at that moment, in fact, jockeying with his dear, dear friend for the best camera angles, was repeating, though in blunter, gutteral tones, ". . . It is a sad, sad day . . ." so that the activists on the steps, including Peter, hand on gun, and Deirdre, fist still clenched, and Kitty, trying her best to avoid being trampled on, thought they were hearing an echo.

"Good morality is good medicine," repeated The Cardinal, he so enjoyed the cleverness of the phrase and wanted the folks at home to be sure to hear it, too; and so evidently did The Mayor, who was quick to echo into the cameras opposite, "Yes, good morality is good medicine . . . and, young man," he added, looking directly down the steps at Peter The Poet, "Didn't your mama ever tell you Cleanliness Is Next To Godliness?" which brought appreciative chuckles from the camera crews.

That Mayor, he never let them down. And this in spite of the fact that he was in a snit because the goings on inside The Cathedral had prevented His Honor from speaking.

"By the way," beamed The Cardinal to the press, "Did you get a copy of my sermon? The one I was trying to deliver, practicing my constitutionally-protected right to religious freedom, before I was so rudely interrupted by these . . . by these . . . Well, *you* fill in the blanks, you are all so far more clever with words . . ."

161

And, as said, since every contingency had been covered in advance, he turned to Brother Francis and murmured, "Here, dear Brother, distribute to the good ladies and gentlemen of our free and glorious Fourth Estate those xeroxes of my homily, since they were deprived of their right to hear it . . ." etc., etc.

". . . before our beloved Cardinal was so rudely interrupted by these know-nothing nincompoops . . ." echoed The Mayor, never at a loss for alliterative invective.

It knocked The Media out.

Once Brother Francis had dispersed the huge stack of the xeroxed sermon to the eagerly grabbing hands of "The Fourth Estate," The Cardinal, in his most oilily smiling voice, had just finished saying (parroted immediately, of course, by The Mayor), "All animosity is so very upsetting," when tiny but powerfully lunged Kitty yelled just about up in his face, she and Deirdre were that close to him by then, "INCLUDING YOUR OWN! YOU INHUMANE HYPOCRITE!"

The Cardinal was so taken aback, he momentarily lost his television smile: he was not used to being called "inhumane"; he was not used to being called "hypocrite" (to his face anyway); he was used to being treated with reverence, especially by The Mayor (all those Catholic votes) and The Media (all those Catholic viewers), as if he were a holy relic.

It was just at that moment that Tom the Trickster let go his banner, its bolts of parachute silk slithering down the gray-stone facade of The Cathedral in a phallic explosion of brilliant red, unveiling, in huge lavender letters, its message of GET HARD ON THE CARDINAL'S BIGOTRY! (a whoop rose from the crowd), just as Peter the Poet, on the left of The Cardinal, was drawing the semi-automatic stealthily but gingerly out of his knapsack, his hand, as always whenever he handled the gun, shaking badly, while Deirdre, advancing doggedly to the right of His Excellency, was set to let go with a roundhouse right, when, with a little help from Asmaralda, who, still in the heart of the swallow and suddenly hearing Big Sister whisper in her ear, "Swallow, no cardinal's worth doing jail time over," with a slap of her wings and a peck of her beak, let the sewn-in ballast stones of the weighty left edge of the banner strike Peter's pistol hand, knocking the gun out of it and sending the weapon clattering down the steps, but not before the pistol went off, the bullet flying wildly, hitting The Cardinal's pompadour, so stiff with Wildroot Cream Oil it was bullet-proof and ricocheted the bullet up into the great bronze doors where it penetrated one of the embossed saints just above The Cardinal's head, leaving The Poet flat-footed and open-mouthed for an instant; while, not a second later, with a swift dive from Asmaralda, the other end of the banner caught Deirdre's mean-looking right, catching her off guard, so that she dropped her clenched fist in the confusion that followed, as the falling broad banner, its weighted end, with another flick of Asmaralda's wings, striking The Cardinal on the forehead and slicing into the carefully coiffed coxcomb of a pompadour, smote it flat, the whole of the cock-shaped banner dropping like a stage curtain in front of the trio, momentarily shielding them from the TV cameras, which were eagerly panning up and down its long length, not to mention also shielding them from the eyes of the police and The Cardinal's and The Mayor's bodyguards.

The Cardinal's clerically-dressed guards hurriedly whipped aside the banner, just as Tom The

Trickster, still strapped to the steeple, snatched from his backpack the several gross of rainbow-hued condoms and tossed handfuls of them over the balustrade, raining them down by the hundreds on the heads of the crowds below (including The Cardinal's), who, like children at a fair, scrambled for them gleefully, suddenly turning the atmosphere of The Demo for the moment into a good-natured game of who could grab the most "prizes." When there were none left, Tom leaned back on his safety belt and clenched both fists triumphantly above his head, to the laughter and applause of the crowd, many of whom now recognized him, before he shimmied down the steeple, unsnapped the belt and, scampering off over the roofs, disappeared from view.

Meanwhile, the bodyguards were hustling the somewhat dazed Cardinal, his immaculately oiled pompadour now a mussed lank of hair fallen in his eyes, back into the vestibule and through the side door leading down into the private passageways beneath The Cathedral that led to the sanctuary of The Chancellory; while Peter The Poet, on his hands and knees, searched frantically for the semi-automatic between the legs of the crowds still milling every which way on The Cathedral steps.

The police SWAT team, positioned on either side of The Cathedral, went immediately into action, some racing down 50th while others raced down 51st Street, all heading to Madison Avenue and the rear of The Chancellory, hoping to cut off The Trickster; while others, tossing up long lengths of climbing rope, most of them missing their targets—obviously they were not as practiced at handling a lasso as Tom, with, of course, an assist from Asmaralda—before they hooked them in the gutters of the steep roof and began their climb up after the culprit.

Meanwhile, at that precise moment, Skint The Skinhead, not to be denied, was just about to hit Deirdre's broad buttocks with his spray can, when Kitty, spotting him, let out a cry. Deirdre swung herself around and, recognizing him as the character who had yelled on the subway and as the one who had snatched her sign away, which he was still clutching like a weapon in his other hand, doubled up her fist again, swung back her arm as far as it would go, and let go with a haymaker that knocked Skint sprawling ass overhead backwards down the steps. As he was falling, she then snatched his spray paint can out of his hand and pointing it in his face, pressed the button.

Kitty wrapped her own slender arms around that massive punching arm, crying out, "My heroine!" while Deirdre, responding to the cheers of all the women crowded round, impulsively lifted, as Tom The Trickster hanging from the steeple had done moments before, her powerful arms over her head in a clenched boxer's victory, at the same time inadvertently lifting the still-clinging Kitty off her feet and high up in the air. From that vantage point, as Skint The Skinhead, now blinded by his very own spray can, staggered dazed and disoriented to his feet, almost tripping over Peter The Poet who was still down on his hands and knees searching for the gun, Kitty snatched the KILL A KOCKSUCKER FOR THE KARDNAL sign out of Skint's hands and broke it over his shaved skull.

The red-faced Skint, in both senses of the word, slunk off unsteadily down the steps, led by the hand by Corkie, who, flat-faced as ever, understood that as soon as they got back to the apartment on Avenue A, she'd get the fucking, and the beating, of her life.

Meanwhile, Tom The Trickster, swifter than the SWAT team, some of whom, with their bulging beer bellies, were noticeably overweight, scurried over the rooftops, also racing toward the rear of The Cathedral to The Chancellory roof, where, once there and reaching the spot where he'd begun his climb a few hours earlier, and where now at that very moment under that very same roof The Cardinal was being helped by his guards into his canopied bed, he swung himself out and over the eaves, and, gripping the rain spout at the corner of the building, slid down it like it was a fire pole. Just instants before the SWAT team on the ground, also red-faced and panting, converged on the block from either side street, he tore off with almost invisible speed south on Madison, racing for the relative safety of the bowels of the subway, before the SWATS had a chance to nab him.

Late that night, back in the tenement on Avenue D, Tom The Trickster, thoroughly exhausted from his long and arduous day, squatted naked— he also believed he did his best thinking naked— under his wrought-iron floor lamp, plotting out his next trick: a scheme to hoist a banner this time from the torch-bearing arm of The Statue of Liberty that would read LIBERATE AIDS RE-SEARCH AND MEDICINE.

While up on the third floor, Deirdre and Kitty, finally drifting off to sleep, lay wrapped in each other's arms on Deirdre's queen-sized mattress, their sides still aching from laughter from every time they had thought of Skint The Skinhead's red face, on the subway ride back from The Cathedral.

Up on the top floor, Peter The Poet, who had arrived home from The Demo only moments before, after fruitlessly spending hours searching for the lost semi-automatic, sat hunched over his rickety writing table, a candle burning at his elbow, the tip of his tongue sticking out one corner of his mouth, while he scratched away with one of his BIC pens on a piece of scrap paper at a long narrative verse entitled "A Day and a Night at the Cathedral," in which he expressed his disappointment at not bumping off The Cardinal but was elated, as is the way with poets, to be finally writing the poem he'd been trying so desperately to write all the wee hours of that morning.

In the rear apartment on the same floor, Asmaralda, who scarcely ever slept, was seated again on her soiled pillow, a fresh bowl of burning herbs smoking up into her nostrils, as, with great frog eyes closed, she murmured, *"Oma, Oma,"* over and over.

Tucked under the pillow, with just its butt end showing, was the semi-automatic Peter had "lost" on the steps of The Cathedral.

Meanwhile, over on Avenue A, Corkie, in a marijuana stupor, lay tangled in the sheets on the mattress on the floor in her and Skint's apartment. She slept alone, since Skint, in his full leather gear, his face turpentine-scrubbed of its red spray paint, had left an hour before for his bouncer's job at The Klub, praying some "dumb fag" showed up at the door that night by mistake. Corkie twitched in her comatose state, her crotch still burning from the pounding Skint had given her. But now, after several joints, she no longer

167

felt it, no longer felt anything, not even the pain in her swollen right eye.

And up on Madison Avenue, his pompadour carefully restored by Brother Francis, The Cardinal, a small bandage on his forehead, lay under the canopy of his bed, at his bedside a huge spray of gladiolas from The Mayor as red as The Mayor's own hair, as red as The Cardinal's own hat, and slept the sleep of the just.

A Note on the Author

Michael Rumaker was born in Philadelphia in 1932, grew up in Southern New Jersey, and was educated at Black Mountain College and Columbia University. His books include the novels *The Butterfly, A Day and a Night at the Baths* (to be published in a German edition in 1993), *My First Satyrnalia,* and *Gringos and Other Stories,* which was recently reissued in a new edition. His one-act play *Queers* was published in Germany as *Schwul.* He teaches creative writing and lesbian and gay studies courses at City College of New York.

This book has been set in Clarendon Light by Graphic Composition, Inc. and printed by Thomson-Shore, Inc.

Designed by Jonathan Greene.